Joseph Hatton

Three Recruits and the Girls They Left Behind Them

A novel. Part 3

Joseph Hatton

Three Recruits and the Girls They Left Behind Them
A novel. Part 3

ISBN/EAN: 9783337065140

Printed in Europe, USA, Canada, Australia, Japan

Cover: Foto ©Andreas Hilbeck / pixelio.de

More available books at **www.hansebooks.com**

THREE RECRUITS

AND

THE GIRLS THEY LEFT BEHIND THEM

A Novel

BY

JOSEPH HATTON

AUTHOR OF

"CLYTIE," "CRUEL LONDON," "THE QUEEN OF BOHEMIA,"
&c., &c.

IN THREE VOLUMES.
VOL. III.

LONDON:
HURST AND BLACKETT, PUBLISHERS,
13, GREAT MARLBOROUGH STREET.
1880.

LONDON :

PRINTED BY DUNCAN MACDONALD, BLENHEIM HOUSE,

BLENHEIM STREET, OXFORD STREET.

BOOK III.

DISCHARGED BY FATE.

Fate steals along with silent tread,
Found oftenest in what least we dread,
Frowns in the storm with angry brow,
But in the sunshine strikes the blow.

COWPER.

THREE RECRUITS.

CHAPTER VIII.

MASKED AND UNMASKED.

Tremble, thou wretch,
That hast within thee undivulged crimes,
Unwhipped of justice.

King Lear.

TOM BERTRAM let the Angel's best hack have her head, and the nag ambled steadily along, while his rider's thoughts travelled to the Home Farm, and the girl he had left behind him, and then

back again to the old days of Grassmoor
and Chesterfield.

It had occurred to him once or twice
that it would perhaps have been better to
have arrived in the village a little earlier.
The good folks might be gone to bed. The
coach was later than he expected, the night
was very dark, though it was not more
than half-past nine.   Judging from his
memories of the past, Farmer Kirk would
be about taking his " night-cap " and smoking his pipe, while Mrs. Kirk sat close by
the candle reading the family Bible.   All
the children would be long since abed, and
there would be a light in Mary's room.
His poor old mother was always in her
chamber in the little Grassmoor farmhouse
of his sister, and so there was no good
speculating about her.   Indeed, there is
no purpose to serve in confessing that his
thoughts were all centred in the Home

Farm, its clean, cosy house-place, its trim garden, its pleasant meadows, its fine-hearted master, its prim and, to him, rather starchy mistress, and its dove-eyed goddess, whose face had haunted him since, like Modus in the play, he had first noticed the brightness of woman's eye.

Tom had no other explanation to give of his coming home at all than was to be found in the magic of that ever-present memory. At night by the camp fire, at morning in the battle, at noon flushed with victory, at evening in hospital, at all hours, under all circumstances, Tom Bertram had seen in his mind's eye the girl he worship-ped; and the band on his arm had nerved him to acts of heroism in the fight, and to patience and endurance under his wounds. No Red-Cross Knight, with his lady's glove in his casque, had ever found more stimu-lus to doughty deeds in a love-token

than had Tom in the memory of Mary
Kirk, and the one little word of hope that
Susan Hardwick had whispered in his ear
at parting.   Yet she had not returned his
love; she had preferred another to him.
It was a strange mad constancy that which
held Tom Bertram's heart; and nothing
would shake it.   Had Mary Kirk been
married to another, her devoted, unsophisticated lover would have nursed his
own blighted hopes and her children possibly at the same time, spending his life in
the village, and coming at last to be called
Daddy, everybody's friend, but more especially the friend of Farmer Kirk's grand-
children.

It was only when he feared that the
sight of him would keep her wounds of
sorrow open; only when he knew that his
voice would perpetually remind her of the

true lover she had lost; only when power-less to save Jacob Marks, and useless as a consoler; that Tom had resolved to cut away the village ties which bound him, and join the army of the King.

"Has she got over her sorrow?" he thought; "young hearts donnat go on pining for ever. How will she receive me? Is there anybody else in the way? No other, if Farmer Kirk has any influence. I'm a maimed man; though my heart's as good as ever; ay, and my arm."

It was a proud thought this last one. Tom little knew how soon it was to be tested.

His thoughts ran quickly ahead now, as he began to recognize even in the darkness certain land-marks on the road. He saw old familiar things in his fancy as he had seen them a thousand times hundreds of miles away. They were realities now. He reflected that in half an hour he would be riding through the long straggling village of Grassmoor.   There would be flickering lights in the windows.   He would hear the ripple of the road-side stream as it fed the watercress and mosses. He would get down to open the farmer's gate.   He would knock at the farmer's door.   The dogs would bark, and the farmer would come to the door himself and open it, a pipe in his hand ! Tom's heart began to beat wildly as he thought of the light in the chamber window over the door.   The nag broke into a gallop as if it had a sudden inspiration of sympathy with its rider.

"Pull up, or you are a dead man !" just as suddenly rang out in a hard firm voice from the middle of the road.

Taken aback for a moment, the challenge, however, acted on Tom's nerves like the word of command.   Quick as thought he was alive to the danger of the situation.

"Why, damn it, man!" he exclaimed, shaking his sword loose in its scabbard, "you don't want to rob a poor soldier who's been fighting for his country?"

It was useless to try to use his pistols, for they were not primed, and he felt that he was covered by the enemy. But, reining his horse about quickly, he drew his sword almost noiselessly.

"Stand, or this moment's your last!"

"Oh, stand be blowed!" said Tom. "I haven't seen real fighting to be dumped by a damned footpad!" and he charged the foe pell-mell.

Daisy was too quick for the lumbering nag from the Angel. She wheeled beautifully, leaving Tom to go plunging half way up the bank by the road-side. But the Angel horse was sturdy and not without pluck, and Tom gathered it upon its legs and was once more combating the foe, his sword swinging above his head, when bang went the enemy's guns one after the other. One of the bullets hit its mark, but the light of the flash showed the figure and attitude of the foe, and happily on the side of Tom's one active eye. Tom almost sprang out of the saddle as he fairly lifted his horse to the charge, and struck down the highwayman with one of those tremendous blows which had so often in the Peninsula demonstrated the value of that superior muscular strength which has carried the British soldier to the very height of his most ambitious hopes.

Riderless in a struggle for the first time, Daisy stood motionless. Then, finding her master did not remount, she trembled in every limb. Tom slipped from his saddle, and was no sooner out of it than his horse turned and started off for Chesterfield as fast as four legs could carry him, his shoes striking fire as he went, and crashing along the road with a noise that awakened the echoes for miles round. Away he went helter-skelter. It was lucky the toll-gate had been left open. Clatter of hoof and rattle of rein and crupper, right along the level road, down Hasland Hill, past the Horns, up Lordsmill Street (people hurried to their doors), round Beetwell Street, straight for the Angel yard, running over a drunken man in the market-place, catching the rein in a pile of tressels and stalls and rattling them over the place ; the runaway horse never stopped until it stood, reeking with foam and blood, at the stable door, for it had been shot in the fleshy part of the neck.

There was a great hubbub at the Angel. The grooms rushed out; so likewise did the guests smoking their evening pipes, the landlord puffing and blowing, Susan Jane's ribbons flying. In less than no time there were " mounting in hot haste " and loading of pistols, and half a dozen men on horseback, including Dick Holmes and a stranger from London, who had been entertaining the company with a fund of racy stories and anecdotes. The stranger had represented himself to be a bagman. He was attired soberly, and seemed to know all about woollen goods and cloths; for between ourselves Mr. Spelter had commenced his career in a hosier and clothier's shop, and knew a great deal about the trade. Before the Chesterfield heroes knew where they were, he had taken charge of the expedition.

" A sowjer—a hofficer I made him out to be," says the groom; "'oss booked for Derby, ordered by guard of Nimrod Coach, paid Miss Susan Jane fifteen bright guineas deposit for 'oss; guard tipped me wink, said he wonnat goin' quite as far as Derby, p'raps not half as fur—goin' to surprise his friends, disbanded soldier."

"Dang me, I shouldn't wonder if it be Tom Bertram, who was expected at the end of the week!" says the landlord.

"Hold the lantern up," says Spelter; "is that local mud?"

"How dost mean?" says the groom.

"Why, where is there mud like that— what part of road?"

"That mud's dust," says the groom— "that mud's sweat, Mester Lundoner, and 'oss is wounded in the neck badly, see thee!"

"Fetch Jerry Bray the Vet.," says the landlord to a bystander, who hurried off for the surgeon.

"If you want to know where 'oss turned

and come home, she's not been away long
enough to get further than dead arches
this side o' Grassmoor," says the groom.

"Was the rider armed?" Spelter asks.

"He wor; he'd a sword, at all events."

"Pistols?"

"I donnat know."

"Sword no good against long, steel-
barrelled pistols—we shall find your customer dead in the road—but we may perhaps understand the private mark of the
villain who's killed him—come, friends—I
know the way."

"You!" they exclaim.

"Yes, every inch of it—experienced
bagman knows every highway in England."

"True," they say; "well, lead on,
mester!"

And the little troop started off at a trot,
presently moving into a gallop, to the

renewed consternation of the little town, whose wondering inhabitants were by this time mostly at their doors and windows.

Meanwhile Tom Bertram, finding his man evidently dying, tried to mount Daisy with a view to seeking assistance. But Daisy would not be mounted. She slewed round and round; she reared; she backed; she plunged; to stand still again the moment Tom desisted.

It was too dark to see what sort of injury the highwayman had sustained, but feeling at the vagabond's head, Tom was satisfied that he had wielded his military sword with powerful effect, and he thanked his good fortune for it, seeing that his own life had been in mortal jeopardy.

He shouted " Hillo! Hi! Murder! Hillo!" as loudly as he could, in the hope of attracting the attention of other wayfarers, at the same time gripping his sword in

case of further attack ; but not a creature
responded; and the few cottage lights away
in the distance were gradually disappearing.

Then he made another attack on Daisy,
and in the midst of a struggle, in which
the gallant little mare had all but suc-
cumbed, Tom felt a sudden giddiness come
over him, a deadly sense of sickness which
was not new to him, since he had been
twice seriously wounded in the field.   He
put his left hand in his breast, and stag-
gered towards the roadside bank, where
the avenging army from Chesterfield found
him lying senseless.

It astonished the bagman's companions,
when they arrived at the scene of the
encounter, to find their self-elected chief
provided with a dark lantern and bandages.

"Always carry them," he said—"never
know what may happen—travellers' companions these—and this."

He took out a small flask and poured a strong dose of brandy into Tom Bertram's mouth, while he unbuttoned his jacket and took off his belt.

"The honest man first," he said—"though I've really most interest in the other—wounded in the breast—not much more than a scratch—force of bullet broken by accoutrements—but bleeding awfully—give me your handkerchief—yes, that's it, Dick Holmes—strap it with belt round shoulders—good—never knew fellow named Dick who was a fool—capital—you shall marry Susan Jane some day—fine girl, Susan Jane—now, then, lift him upon quietest horse there is—one sit behind—hold him up—another lead—take him to nearest house."

"To Farmer Kirk's," said several voices at once.

VOL. III.   C

"That ain't nearest," said Spelter, quickly.

"Not much in it as to distance, and will get best attention there," said Dick Holmes, who, being in love himself, had a fellow-feeling for Tom, whose particular weakness in regard to the Kirk family was a matter of notoriety.

"All right—take charge, Dick—you are promoted to Captain—see the soldier safe inside Kirk's house—one of you other gentlemen ride on with all speed to the Home Farm and prepare them for hospital work —that's it—there you are, you see!"

Away went the young tradesman whom we have previously met, clattering off to Kirk's, Dick Holmes and another following with Tom, whom the rider held partly in his arms, administering now and then a dose from the bagman's flask, which presently began to have the desired effect of rousing Tom out of the stupor which loss of blood had brought on.

"Now, then," said the supposed bagman, turning to the other object in the road, and flashing his light on Daisy.

"Why, that's owd Short's mare!" exclaimed one of the remaining members of Spelter's escort.

"And, by heaven, that's Short himsen!" he said, as Spelter removed the mask and discovered the highwayman's pale face, with its eyes half opened, its mouth rigid.

"I'd have bet ten guineas on it!" exclaimed Spelter, "and I'd have stood fifty if he'd been as little hurt as the soldier."

The two men from Chesterfield, who knew Short well, stood as still as Daisy herself.

"Dead as mutton—wish he was as wholesome—soldier has a strong arm and a good sword—cut him clean through the neck—worthy of Life-Guardsman Shaw— in the dark, too—better die like this than have Jack Ketch slinging his weapon at you—we'll carry him home, gentlemen— —the canting scoundrel!"

Daisy lowered her head as they began to raise her master. She made no resistance when Spelter laid his hand upon the rein close by her mouth. She stood as quiet as a lamb while they lifted the lifeless body on her back.

" Knew I should have him," said Spelter, as the *cortége* moved off—" hard lines to pick him up like this—just my luck—in at the death, it's true—but I had arranged a proper exit for him—confound that long sword !"

" Who the devil are *you*, then ?" asked the man who was walking by Spelter's side and leading Daisy.

"You will pity me when I tell you," he replied.

"You are not a bagman, then?"

"Do I look like one?"

"Yes."

"Thank you—compliment to my disguise—and my acting—think I must go on the stage."

"Perhaps you are also one of the chaps as wears masks and does business on highway," rejoined the other.

"No," was the answer; "I wear a mask, but not Short's kind--he wore a mask I could never stomach—successful mask, too —-religion—a mask and a cloak too, that —do anything behind 'em when they are worn cleverly—no, I'm an honest man!"

"Who are you, then? You shan't budge another inch till you tell us," said the questioner, laying his hand on Daisy's bridle; "a whipper-snapper like you!

Let's have no more on it, out with it!"

"I will, you ought to know—no right to trespass longer on your good nature —have you ever heard of a Bow Street runner?"

"Yes, course we have; do you think we be fools?"

"Of Dick Spelter?"

"King of Bow Street runners!" exclaimed the interrogator.

"You flatter me."

"You are not him?"

"I am," said Spelter.

"The devil!" remarked the other man, speaking for the first time during the whole proceeding.

CHAPTER IX.

A HERO IN CLOVER.

"None without hope e'er loved the brightest fair,
  But Love can hope where Reason would despair."
                                    LYTTLETON.

TOM BERTRAM had a night of strange rest, so quiet was it, so calm. He was himself now and then, but when he was most himself he seemed most at sea. When he was most himself he concluded most emphatically in his own wandering mind that he was in the temporary hospital outside Paris, being nursed by those soft-footed Sisters of Mercy to whom he may be said to have owed his life.

From that time the past was like a dream. His leaving Paris, his journey by sea, his arrival at Dover, his conversation with the guard of the London coach, his little purchases in the metropolis, his starting homewards, his ride out of Chesterfield. It was all a dream, leading up to a skirmish with the enemy, to a surprise of picquets, an ambush, a fight, and a wound.

But in the morning all these mists were cleared away. The doctor had been, and pronounced Tom's hurt of no serious account. Loss of blood had been and was Tom's chief trouble. He would soon get over that. He was to be kept quiet.

Tom put his hand into Farmer Kirk's, and the two strong men wept like children.

"You monnat talk much, my lad," said Kirk.

"It's all straight, eh?" Tom replied,

"I am not dreaming, eh? It's you, farmer?"

"Ah, lad, it's me, true enough."

"Thank God!" said Tom; "ay, thank God! for He's been merciful to me."

"He's good to them as deserves it, Tom; but you monnat get excited, lad."

"It would have been hard, after all, to come home and be shot down like a dog in sight of Grassmoor!" said Tom.

"Ah, lad, it would; but here's missus, thou must keep quiet."

"Yes, don't say too much," said Mrs. Kirk; "sit up, lad, and take this."

Tom sat up. The farmer packed the pillows behind him. Mrs. Kirk handed him a basin of mutton broth.

"Eh, Mrs. Kirk, it's right good of you to be taking care on me like this," said Tom.

"It would be right mean if we didn't

help thee, lad; don't fret on that score; it's a pleasure to us."

"Thank you. Does my owd mother know?"

"Ay, all village knows, all country will by end of week; there, now, lie down and donnat think about it. And, farmer, if you must stay in the room, sit down by fire and say nowt."

Tom and the farmer obeyed the head-nurse. The under-nurse was on the stairs outside.

"Well, mother," she whispered, "how is he now?"

"Ever so much better; he'll soon be well if thy father will only stop talking to him."

"Has he asked after me?"

"Not as I know on."

"Oh!" said Mary, following her mother into the house-place.

" He asked about his mother."

"Don't you think he would like to see me ?"

"Maybe; but farmer agrees with me he'd better not just yet !"

" Oh ! How does he look, mother ?"

" Worn, and tired, and ill."

"Poor fellow ! And his eye, mother ?"

"Disfigured, certainly, but not much."

" Not much ? Is there a patch on it ?"

"No, it doesn't look much different to the other, only sight is gone."

"Really !"

" He says if he'd had two eyes, he'd a been a dead man this day."

" Why, mother ?"

" Because his sight would have wandered; he got that murdering villain away from blind side, and he can see such a lot and look so hard, only having one."

"Oh! that is a good thing, is it not, mother?"

"Ah, it is, lass; misfortunes are good things sometimes."

" Does he look much older?"

"A year or two."

" His hair isn't grey?"

"Grey, no! It's as brown and glossy as ever, as far as I can mak' out."

"I'm glad of that. Poor fellow, what a deal of trouble he has had!"

"He has so!" said Mrs. Kirk; " but Heaven selected him."

"Yes? What for?"

"To minister justice."

" Yes?"

" He'd never have been found out if God hadn't tore mask off, and smote him with the sword of Tom Bertram!" said Mrs. Kirk, pausing in her work and looking at Mary.

"That man Short, you mean!" said Mary, shuddering, and looking round as if she feared he might be at her elbow.

"Devil, not man, Mary!" said her mother; "but the justice of heaven has found him, late in the day, perhaps; earthly justice would never have done it."

"How awful it all is!" said Mary, laying her head upon her mother's shoulder.

A week later, in the afternoon, Tom was dressed and sitting by the fire downstairs. In a day or two he would be able to go out and see his mother. He had been allowed to talk of Mary, and she had sent him a bunch of fresh flowers every morning. She had seen him, though he had not seen her. Her mother had allowed her to look in upon him while he slept. The doctor, who knew the situation fully, had positively forbidden that he should see Miss Kirk under a week.

At last the happy hour came. Mrs. Kirk had contrived that no one should witness the meeting. Mary was by his side before he could rise from his chair to receive her.

" No, you must sit still, Tom," she said, taking his hand; "sit quite still while I talk to you."

"You might as well ask wind to be still when it's blowing big guns," said Tom, standing up. "Mary! oh, Mary!"

" Tom!" said the girl, her heart beating wildly.

How she came the next moment to be sobbing in his arms she can never make out to this day; but her nerves had been so tried, she used to say in after-years, when speaking of the incident, that she quite lost her head: what with the death of Lord Ellerbie, the return of Mr. North, the justice of heaven on Short, and the justification of poor Jacob Marks, a young girl might well be excused for giving way to her feelings under these trying circumstances, when they were capped by meeting Tom Bertram again. For if ever girl had a true and devoted lover, Mary Kirk had in Tom Bertram.

They were sitting by the fire talking, the farmer, Mrs. Kirk, Tom, and Mary, in the twilight, when my lady's coach that had been made in Paris pulled up in the road outside the garden, and, before anyone could go out to receive her, the Countess of Ellerbie was in the room.

"A truly happy family!" said Susan; "glad to see you all; don't get up one of you; yes, Tom Bertram may."

Tom stood forward, looking a little sheepishly at the splendid woman who addressed him; for Susan was radiant, though in deep mourning, her eyes as bright as the diamonds that fastened her cloak.

Since Tom had last seen her she had become a woman. She had changed even more than Mary had. Born to command, Susan carried her new dignity with an easy aristocratic grace. She would have looked a lady had you dressed her in rags. A Countess, she looked the picture of a Queen.

"Let me see the man who is as valiant in peace as in war, and whose heart has never wavered in his devotion!" said the Countess. "Give me your hand, Tom!"

The bashful hero put out his hand. Susan laid hers in his great palm.

"Squeeze it, Tom! You did when we parted."

"God bless you!" said Tom, pressing her hand; "and you said she should not forget me. Mr. North said you would keep your word."

"Never mind Mr. North," answered the Countess. "What did you do with the keepsake I gave you?"

"Ay, Mary," said Tom, turning to the blushing girl by his side, "it was that as saved me. Oliver North said it was talisman against fire and sword."

"What do you mean, Tom?" asked Mary.

"Why, this!" he said, turning up the sleeve of his right arm.

"The bracelet I gave to Susan!" said Mary, looking at the Countess.

"The bracelet *I* gave to Tom," said the Countess. "Come and kiss me, Mary! Tom may kiss my hand."

Mary was in the Countess's arms the next moment, and while Susan fondled her,

and stroked her wavy hair, she turned to
Tom, trying all the time to appear calm
and collected, and asked, "What did North
say?"

"I towd him you said Mary should not
forget me, and he said, 'Then depend on
it she won't—Miss Hardwick will keep her
word.'"

"Yes, and something else you said?"

"About this bracelet? He said he envied
me the token, and he called it a talisman,
and so it has been, or else I'd never have
been here to see this happy and blessed
day."

"A little thing comforts one sometimes,
Tom," said Susan; "it is a satisfaction to
know that one has kept small promises if
one has broken great ones! Ah! well,
I must be content to see other people
happy. There, let us all sit down and talk;
I have come to tea, Mrs. Kirk."

What a tea-party it was! Never, surely, had the world seen a countess so condescending and so sweet!

BOOK IV.

THE RECKONING.

"If you ever listen to David's harp you shall hear
as many hearse-like airs as carols; and the pencil of
the Holy Spirit hath laboured more in describing the
affliction of Job than the felicities of Solomon. Prosperity is not without many fears and disasters; and
Adversity is not without comforts and hopes. We see
in needleworks and embroideries, it is more pleasing to
have a lively work upon a sad and solemn ground than
to have dark and melancholy work upon a lightsome
ground : Judge therefore of the pleasures of the heart
by the pleasures of the eye. Certainly virtue is like
precious odours, most fragrant when they are crushed;
for Prosperity doth best discover Vice, but Adversity
doth best discover Virtue."—LORD BACON.

CHAPTER I.

THE RETURNED PRODIGAL.

Gayer insects fluttering by
Ne'er droop the wing o'er those that die,
And lovelier things have mercy shown
To every failing but their own,
And every woe a tear may claim,
Except an erring sister's shame.

BYRON.

MAJOR GEORGE WINGFIELD, released from duty with the army of occupation in France, having in his pocket a considerable sum for arrears of pay and a long leave, sat in the dull wainscoted coffee-room of an hotel in the neighbour-

hood of Piccadilly, where the Dover coach
had deposited him. Hard service had
seasoned the boyish beauty of the face
which had looked love into the eyes of
Jessie Burns and defiance into those of his
father. It had not worn him as it had
Oliver North. He looked strong and full
of health, his fair complexion reddened by
exposure to the weather and the heat of
the sun, his broad chest more expansive
than ever, his limbs clean cut and firmly
knit. He wore his moustache, which
drooped luxuriantly over his full red lips.
A man now, George was not altered except to this extent : A picture of robust
youth when he drew his sword to march
with his company that autumn morning in
the old Derbyshire market-place, he was
now that same picture finished, developed
into manhood.

Wearing loose undress uniform, people turned to look at him in the London streets; for he had been in town some weeks, having important financial business to settle with the War Office, and other duties belonging to the close of a long and important military service.

At Dover he had sat down and composed a long and serious letter to his father, asking to be received at the Vicarage as of old with open arms, begging his father to let bygones be bygones. "I deeply regret and deplore the past, sir," he wrote, "and would atone to the full, if I knew how. I trust that my honest endeavours to carry the family name unsullied through the dangers of a great war have in a measure removed from your mind the recollection of the folly of my youth: this has been a source of continual reproach to me when I have looked back, and I should have suffered beyond endurance, had I not felt that in your heart you could not hold me in continual abhorrence, and had I not also been equally assured of my mother's prayers." Then he referred to the pleasant days of his boyhood, to his father's great charges in respect of his education, thanking the Vicar for all this and for his noble example of courage and rectitude, and concluded by saying, "If one regret more than having parted from you in anger has troubled me, it has been that I did not obey your command and marry as you wished. That poor loving girl has been always in my mind, and I never considered that I esteemed her sufficient to make her my wife until I was far beyond reach of her. I trust, sir, you have been a father to her, as you declared you would be, and that it is well with her, for great was her trouble, and sore her need. God forgive me for it! Touching what passed between myself and Miss Manners, I leave that to be ordered as you may think best for her happiness and your own honour."

It was an honest, manly letter, the work of one who had been tried; who had been face to face with death many a time; who had looked on scenes of slaughter and misery; who had witnessed acts of heroism in men as well as in women; who had seen wonders of devotion and self-sacrifice among the daughters of Spain and France; and who had learnt higher and nobler lessons from war than most men who had fought their way from Madrid to Vitoria, from Vitoria to Waterloo, from Waterloo to Paris. George's was a sociable nature, and when he left home the lad did not know how home memories would cling to him, how his heart would go back to the vicarage, to his father and mother, and to that unsophisticated, unthinking girl, with her musical Scotch accent and her soft winning ways. He thought himself a "devil of a fellow," a sort of Captain Plume, a lady-killer, a lad of mettle, a soldier who was going forth to make conquest of hearts, as well as of forts and fields, a Don Juan and a Hector in one; instead of which he had gradually discovered that he was just an average honest, thoughtless, brave young Englishman, with, on the whole, more than an average sense of his moral and religious responsibilities; and, what is more, that, instead of his having made a conquest of the pretty little lassie at the Post Office under the shadow of the crooked spire, she had made a conquest of him. He had lain many a night thinking of her, and almost cursing himself that he had not married her.

Sandy Burns, the bare mention of

whom as a sort of relation had turned his stomach in that last interview with his father, had long since ceased to be regarded except with the respect due to the father of the girl he really loved. George was changed indeed, and yet he might have argued that he had not changed at all; that he was a raw, inexperienced, selfish youth at Chesterfield, since which time the innate good in him had come out, had developed, had grown with his manhood, to the necessary annihilation of those vicious qualities which he had in his greenness imagined worthy and manly.

As he had neared the white cliffs of Albion, his longing to see Jessie again had taken hold of him with increasing power. "I am coming back, my own little Jessie; I told you I should," he had written before embarking at Calais, "and you will find me, though now a Major—mark you, a

Major, Jessie—still the same old affectionate George."

He had asked his father to address his
reply to the hotel at which he should stay
in London, and the Vicar did so, but not
until he had taken time to consider well
what he should say, and his wife had agreed
with him that the truth and the whole truth
was the best at all times. So the Vicar
had written as follows :—

"MY DEAR SON,—For so you are, George,
and always have been, notwithstanding
the grief I did suffer under, long and sore,
and thy mother likewise, from thy sin and
disobedience. That said, give me leave to
confess thy letter hath given me and thy
worthy mother great joy, and it is a comfort to me to feel that as a soldier you
have done credit to the country that bred
you, and to the name you bear.

"You have done more than carry your sword with honour, my son—you have conquered yourself. *Patitur qui vincit:* But he becomes strong, and the truth will not be able to cast him down, for even as we sow shall we reap. Prepare, then, to receive ill news with that which is good. As for me and thy mother, we stretch our arms out to thee, and our free and full forgiveness goes to thee with this letter. Thy father's house is thy due resting-place, and the fatted calf shall be killed.

"Yet must the news hereof which thy mother thinketh with me proper for thee to know be of sadness, since your letter speaks of Jessie Burns, the mother of your child. God is good, and she may yet live; but 'tis four years and some weeks since sight of her or report of her has gladdened Sandy or myself. Sore beset with the women of this town, who could not

forgive her the sin thou hadst put upon
her, she fled the virtuous furies, a plague
upon them, and has been lost to us as if
she had died. I fear me Sandy Burns
was hard upon her—in truth, I know he
was, and he has not prospered; from sickness to drink and to the loss of his employment brought him to the humble position of our gardener here at the Vicarage,
but this day he is transferred to a friend's
employment in the Peak, whither he goeth
by the coach, as thy mother advised it
were best he be not in the way when we
welcome thee home.

"Replying to thy inquiries as touching
Miss Manners, she, with my full consent,
married the Yorkshire baronet who, for a
time, was much concerned at the prospect
of being cast off by her. He is a good
husband, she a true and happy wife, and
they do live on his estate in the East

Riding of the great county of the North, and are like to have numerous successors to their wealth. So may heaven prosper them in their love and estates! In which prayer it rejoiceth us to know thou wilt concur.

"In this letter there mingles, as in life, good and ill, joy and sorrow. Bear both as thou hast borne thine honour in the battle-field, and come home with all speed to a father's heart and to a mother's arms. And know, my son, that thy mother hath recovered much of her former health, and doth now share the exercise and delight of the household duties. Be cheered. They have brought your letter addressed to Jessie to the Vicarage. She was most unfortunate, and, though happiness in marriage is found among equals of birth and station, it had pleased thee, George, to make her thy equal, and it may be within the possibility of things that the report in the *Gazettes* and journals of your return may induce her, if she be living and in honour as I truly think if in life, to disclose her retreat and condition, and as Horace hath it—

> ' Deus hæc fortasse benignâ
> Reducet in sedem vice.'

" From your affectionate father and with his blessing.

" NORMANBY WINGFIELD."

It was a heavy blow to George this terrible news concerning Jessie. He sat without moving for half-an-hour with his father's letter in his hand, and then he read it again and again. The brave little heart, he thought, how it had gone forth from the cruel place. He could understand how Jessie, in her fearless way, had turned her back on the canting hypocritical town! What names he called it in his silent agony and passion, sitting there in the unsympathetic coffee-room of the old tavern, forgetting for the moment that he had been more cruel than the town of his nativity! But the sting of his father's letter came home to him presently. Not all the honey which enshrouded it had any sweetness for him. And his child! With what strange sensations of fear and dread, of love and longing, he read that passage of his father's narrative, the story of the wrong he had done the girl he had professed to love only to seek her ruin; and to whom he found his fondest hopes and desires clinging when seas and battle-fields rolled and jarred between him and the pretty stranger whom Fortune had lodged within his influence and power.

There was madness in the thought that his child might be living in poverty and

E 2

wretchedness, its mother enduring un-
heard-of privations. But there was a
faint gleam of hope in this madness,
which, however, only glimmered for a
moment, to fall dead at the suggestion that
Jessie no longer lived. He sat and
thought of every conceivable thing she
might have done, and his mind wandered
to Miller's Dale, the wayside inn, and the
kindly landlady there. Thither he had
advised her to go if she should not be well
treated at home. The only thought that
gave him one drop of comfort and patience
was the remembrance that he had forced a
sum of money upon her at parting. Yet
surely in the search the Vicar would have
instituted, the little fishing-station on the
Derbyshire Wye had not escaped notice.
Then again it might. The vales of Derbyshire were *terra incognito* to half Chesterfield, and few persons came and went in

that shady retreat whither Jessie, supposed to be on a visit to relations far
away, had accompanied her lover one
never-to-be-forgotten happy summer. What
would he have given now to recall it, to
blot it out, and to have left Jessie in her
innocence at home, or have been ruled by
his father and made her the Vicar's daughter! How generous, how noble, he thought
now was his father's conduct compared
with his own. A man proud of his blood,
a soldier once high in command, and now,
as he had said, a soldier of Christ, he had
deigned to stoop even so low as to call
Sandy Burns brother; yet had he, his
degenerate son, thought it a fine thing
to leave the poor pretty unselfish girl and
plume his hat for other conquests, for fresh
fields and pastures new!

George's love burned fiercer now for the
check it encountered, and his debasement,

in his own estimation filled him with a passionate sorrow, a mad affliction of remorse. He buckled on his sword and went out. Walking is a relief to an overwrought mind, and it helps a man to think. When a certain great author encountered his first great trouble in life, he started off and walked twenty miles without stopping. George Wingfield felt a similar impulse. He gratified it. At the same time he resolved all manner of schemes for the discovery of Jessie Burns. Alive and still true to him, he would marry her. Dead, he would raise a monument to her. He hoped that she would find in her child an incentive to live, an inducement to obtain employment, and also a comfort, he thought. Perhaps she had fallen into benevolent hands. Some kindly-disposed lady had taken compassion on her. Oh!

if she were only alive and well under some hospitable roof, how he would reward her for her sufferings, how grateful he would be to her new friends ! That curmudgeon, her contemptible father, it was wise in the Vicar to send him away ! The idea that she might have found an asylum in the Derbyshire valley near Buxton was dissipated on reflection; but, while he was walking and thinking, he turned into the office of the Chief of Police, and consulted that astute official, who, after a short inquiry connected with the detective department of the force, offered to send a messenger down into the country, where he would at the present moment have the advice of perhaps the most capable officer in the service, who was engaged in another matter on the spot.

The suspicious death, or the murder, of

Lord Ellerbie on the day of his marriage was news to George Wingfield, who had heard nothing of Oliver North for a long time, except that he had been struck out of the Army List, and the fact of Susan Hardwick's marriage now convinced him that his brave comrade was indeed dead. This for the moment put aside his own trouble. After all, death was more dreadful than his own living sorrow. Though George had seen the grim monster in every shape, once outside the sweep of his darts he rejoiced in life. He was strong, full-blooded, of genial instincts, and he only scorned death when he was fighting his country's enemies. He eagerly engaged the services of the police, and the messenger was ordered to proceed to Chesterfield by the next coach, take counsel with Mr. Spelter, make every inquiry as to Miss Burns's disappearance, and report to

London, meanwhile extending his personal inquiries to the neighbourhood of Miller's Dale and Buxton.

Conscious that he had taken the promptest and most available means of instituting a search for Jessie and her child, Major Wingfield walked with a more hopeful and elastic tread, though Oliver North and Susan Hardwick ran gloomily in his thoughts. The suspicious death of Lord Ellerbie! Had Scruton succeeded, then? He had not thought to ask the question. If that swashbuckling knave was now the Earl, so much more reason, he thought, for him to hate Chesterfield, and resolve not to live there when he found Jessie. He knew nothing of the duly reported death of Scruton, the epitaphs at Brackenbury and Chesterfield. No such good news as that entered into his hopes; for in his own experience, though death has the credit of being no respecter of persons, he had seen the best fellows fall first. In all the early battles of the Peninsula the young and brave and good comrades, it seemed to him, were invariably selected for the list of killed. It would be quite within his view that Scruton should be alive and North dead, that he himself, for that matter, should come home with only a few scratches and a scalp wound or two, while Tom Bertram should have long weary spells in hospitals, and lose an eye. "But give me the chance to atone," he said to himself, "and I *will* atone!"

He had scarcely given a thought about whither his steps were carrying him since he had retained the services of the police, though he had already excited some attention among the belles and exquisites of the Park. His absent manner, his long, swinging stride, his stalwart figure and bronzed face, and his generally unstudied, yet fine soldierly gait made him quite a figure in the Park; though he was in competition with the Persian Ambassador of the time, who used to ride a white Arabian steed, gaily caparisoned, but not more showily arrayed than himself. History repeats itself. One year it is the Ambassador, with a fair Circassian in his train, who excites the nation of England to a wild pitch of curiosity; the century wanes, and the Shah himself dazzles us with his gems, and fires feminine curiosity, not to say masculine envy, with his trinity of veiled and therefore beautiful wives. Both the one and the other went home utterly stupefied with what they had seen, the last visitor more bewildered than the other; for in his notes on the streets of modern London, the Shah explains that the police officers, who administer and control the traffic, are selected for their handsome figures from the upper classes, and that to insult one of them the penalty is death.

The past and the present are curiously linked in all departments of life. To-day in artistic circles the ladies are dressing very much after the fashion of the latter days of the eighteenth century, which was the mode adopted by Susan Hardwick, Mary Kirk, and Jessie Burns at the commencement of this present history; but they were necessarily behind the metropolis, and happily so, for London had left off the short, stayless waist of Susan Hardwick in our first picture of that tantalising beauty under the elms by her father's door, and had revived that system of tight lacing which obtains in the present day, to the utter destruction of health and beauty.

The Park when Major Wingfield pro-

menaded there, with his long stride and
his thoughtful face, was a picture of
strange *outré* dresses, male and female,
grotesque poke bonnets, tall strange hats,
wasp waists, and sandalled shoes; for men,
short blue coats, tight trousers, narrow-
brimmed tall hats, cocked over the nose,
but not so as to hide an oiled love-lock on
the left temple. Our women show an inclination to follow the changes which began
in 1760, when Paris adopted the semi-
classic robes of Greece, which, by imi-
tation and adaptation, became in England the short-waisted, low-necked, short-
sleeved clinging gown of an English lady
of fashion in the first days of the present
century, and which governed country belles
and county ladies long after the *mode* had
merged in the metropolis into tight lacing and other extremes. Fashions were
slow to change in the country districts of

our fathers, and Hardwick, Kirk, Mrs. Kirk, the Vicar, and their families with slight modifications clung to the habits of dress and manner which obtained in the days of Goldsmith and Dr. Johnson, with the exception of that " baby-waist " gown of Miss Hardwick, which was a slight advance on the time, attributable to Susan's occasional studies of *The Lady's Monthly Museum* of the period.

The country for many years was as little influenced by the vagaries of fashion in London as it was by the wicked stucco reign of Nash in the matter of street and domestic architecture; and so if you would fully realise the days in which this history moves, with the dresses of the period and the bricks and mortar of the time, you must fill your mind with reminiscences of the snug picturesque houses of the eight-eenth century which modern architects are

reviving at Kensington, Hampstead, and
in other directions; you must think of the
old village greens and their fringes of ivy-
coloured houses, with diamond window
panes; you must picture the market-places
of Nottingham, Derby, and Chesterfield
with their stone piazzas, their bow-window-
ed shops, and their canvas-covered stalls;
you must picture Derbyshire before railway
trains, when Buxton was in its infancy,
when the roadside inns in the Peak were
plain, comfortable-looking houses, often
built of local stone quarried in the neighbourhood; when a drive through the hills
and dales of the famous Midland county
was free from the everlasting reek of the
limekiln, the meadow-blasting hand of the
miner, and the screech of the locomotive;
and yet for all this change you have only
to look back from seventy to eighty years.
In the matter of dress, you could hardly

have any more picturesque guide than *The Mad Dog* illustrations of Caldecott, issued in the present year of grace; nor could you have a better example of the educational and art progress of these days than in a comparison of the children's literature of now and then as exemplified in the toy-books of 1879 and those of 1800. And yet, strange to say, we have tolerated all these years the ghastliest change from the picturesque to the ugly, in the matter of architecture, that ever afflicted a nation. It was said of a great emperor that he found Rome a city of stone and left it a city of marble, in reference to which it has been said of Nash that he found London a city of brick and left it a city of stucco. Happily an old English revival has set in, and if you would try to realize the rural and provincial England of these districts where local building-stone was not abun-

dant you have only in fancy to put Caldecott's men and women into Shaw's houses,
reducing the ornamentation of the latter
and toning down the colours with age, to
find yourself at home a hundred years and
more ago ; while thinking of the scenes in
which this present history passes you will
scatter here and there the stone-built
houses of the Peak with the red-tiled and
the thatched buildings of Chesterfield, the
low straggling homesteads of Grassmoor,
and the lichen-covered walls of Brackenbury. As for the justification of the
romance of our history, and what may be
called its improbabilities, the real story of
the times gives ample warrant, the records
of old families equally startling revela-
tions, and the Newgate Calender even
sadder episodes than that of the Miller
and his Men here set forth.

For which personal and explanatory aside,

the author tenders his apologies, and forthwith follows Major George Wingfield to his
hotel, where, after some necessary refresh-
ment, the returned warrior retires to his
own apartment to re-read his father's
letter and chafe against the unexpected
obstacle to the realization of his hopes.
He was glad to learn that at all events he
had not blighted the career of Miss Manners. It was some little consolation to
know that she was settled, if not happy;
for George doubted whether that under-
sized, common little Yorkshire baronet
could suffice for the happiness of any
woman, much less a refined, delicate-
minded woman such as the Vicar's ward.
But George made no allowance for the
pleasant fulfilment of duty which belonged
to the station in life of her Yorkshire lady-
ship. Miss Manners had always been
accustomed to take a leading part in the

parochial work of the Chesterfield Vicarage; she would all the more appreciate the
extended and higher influences appertain-
ing to the lady who presided over the
domestic administration of large estates
with fat livings in her husband's gift and
wide miscellaneous patronage in her own.

George flung himself upon a sofa and
thought *and* thought; picturing in his mind
all his career from his boyish days upwards, his battles at school, his contests at
college, his hair-breadth escapes in Spain,
his almost miraculous salvation at Waterloo; and amidst all the scenes as he came
and went he saw a fair smiling face, with
white teeth and firm rosy cheeks, and reddish wavy hair. If Fate had ordained that
he should be punished by the fanning of
his passion at this time, and the augmenta-
tion of Jessie's attractions, the returned
soldier could not have suffered more than

he did.   The responsibility of pater-
nity, too, made strange claims upon his
fancy.   He wondered that he had never
before thought of this additional link between Jessie and himself, for, though he
had insisted upon her taking his purse for
the reason acknowledged between them,
he had never, until his father's letter was
before him, realised that he might have a
child also to greet him on his return.   Was
it a girl or boy?   With all the right and
proper impulses that could possibly govern
a man under the circumstances, it seemed
to him peculiarly hard that Providence
should delay even a moment the opportunity of atonement.

It was fitting, however, that a man who
had left the pretty devoted girl so heart-
lessly as George Wingfield had left Jessie
should smart for his perfidy, and it was
quite in keeping with the practical unsym-

pathetic character of the police mind that
it should invent for him the cruellest pos-
sibilities. He was presently aroused from
his reflection by a visit from an officer who
had called, with his chief's compliments, to
inform him that on a certain Friday four
years previously the bodies of a young
woman and a female child were found
floating in the Thames near London Bridge.
The remains had never been identified, and
they had been buried at the cost of the
Poor Law Union of the parish in which
they were discovered. From the evidence
of certain articles found on the bodies, it
was believed that the mother had come up
to London from some country district,
possibly to conceal her shame and trouble,
which in the end, coupled with poverty,
had been too much for her, and she had
sought peace in the river.

George's heart sickened as the officer

told his story, and suggested that his chief feared these were the persons for whom he was in search. For some minutes he could not speak. His hands trembled as he buried his face in them, trying in vain to control his emotions. He recovered with an effort, and cross-examined the officer.

"Were no inquiries made after the woman and her child?"

"Yes, many."

"Did anyone inspect the remains?"

"They were almost beyond the possibility of identification."

George shuddered, and standing up leaned his head against the mantelshelf.

"Her clothing?"

"It was laid out for inspection, with the trinkets found on the body."

"And yet she was not identified?"

"No."

" Did anyone come up from Chester-field ?"

He asked this question with eagerness, his voice trembling, as he feared for the answer.

" I cannot tell."

" The colour of her hair ?"

" A reddish brown."

" What effect would the water have on dark red hair ?"

" It is hard to say."

George pressed his hand on his heart and paced the room.

" Have you a record of the people who saw her ?"

" Yes, I should say so."

" And her clothes—are they preserved ?"

" Oh, yes."

" Her trinkets ?"

" Yes, sir."

" Can I see them ?"

"No doubt of it."

"Now?"

"I should say so."

"At once?"

"If you will come along with me."

"If I will!" said George, rushing to the bell and ringing it furiously; "a hackney coach will take us more quickly than we can walk?"

"I think not, sir."

"Come, then, we will go immediately."

A servant entered the room in haste.

"This gentleman will return," said the Major; "serve him with whatever he may desire at my expense."

The officer bowed.

"Forgive the hastiness of my poor effort at hospitality," said George; "*you* will have time to forget this little incident over a bottle by-and-by. God knows what may become of me!"

CHAPTER II.

LITTLE GEORGE, MAJOR GEORGE, AND KING GEORGE.

In fine, this same London is a strange, incongruous chaos of the most astounding riches and prodigious poverty—of feverish ambition and apathetic despair—of the highest charity and the darkest crime; the great focus of human emotion—the scene of countless struggles, failures, and successes, where the very best and the very worst types of civilised society are found to prevail—where there are more houses and more houseless, more feasting and more starvation, more philanthropy and more bitter stony-heartedness, than in any other spot in the world.

MAYHEW's *World of London.*

THE trinkets were *not* Jessie's, nor was the wearing apparel anything like that which she had worn. Indeed, George

Wingfield had come away from the awful
ordeal of the police lumber-room convinced
that the poor creatures who had been found
in the river were not the darlings he had
longed to find. But it was a sorry sight,
the clothing of the unknown victims who
had sought violent relief from the perfidy
of man and the uncharitableness of woman !
The place altogether was the most melancholy apartment it had ever been his lot to
enter ; yet he had seen war in all its hideous shapes ; siege of fort and town, sack
of cottage and palace, the dying and the
dead prone among their household gods.
The police store-room was full of reminiscences of death and crime, the repository
of the murderer's knife, the suicide's pistol,
the burglar's tools, relics of undiscovered
crimes, and ghastly proofs of deeds for
which men and women had been hanged ;

some, too, with the additional horror of being drawn and quartered.

It was from among this blood-curdling collection of things that the bundle, ticketed and dated, was brought out for George to see if the clothes belonged to Jessie Burns. No room of the dead in any Spanish house over which the French armies had swept in victory and in retreat had ever affected him so much as the sight of that bundle and the child's frock and little shoes when the officer spread them out before him. Even while he was convinced that the sad relics did not morally put upon him the crime of murder, he went away haunted with that frock and shoes. Some other poor woman had suffered as Jessie may have suffered for aught he knew. Some other unfortunate child had gone down under the dark waters as his may have gone for aught he knew. The responsibility of that little life preyed on him bitterly.

But he would hope for the best, and he would leave no stone unturned to find the fugitives.

Having sought out a solicitor, whom the police had recommended as a reliable person, he had delivered to him a complete description of Jessie, instructing him to offer a reward for her discovery, and to put himself in communication with the police in the affair, and report to him as long as he remained in town, and after that to the Vicarage at Chesterfield. He had resolved, the moment his business with the Minister of War and the Commander-in-Chief was settled, to go home and begin his inquiry himself at the fountain head.

In the height of his troubles he did not forget the cheering news about his mother.

She was no longer an invalid confined to
her room. She would be downstairs to
receive him. It was in his thoughts that
he would take her a present from London;
and, as he was passing a silk-merchant's
shop the day following his visit to the
police chamber of horrors, he remembered
that in the days when his mother was an
active woman her favourite gown was a
black silk, as stiff as a board, a splendid
material that rustled like a ship's sails in a
gale of wind.

"She shall have the stiffest and best
that money can buy," thought George, as
he entered the shop, through a pair of
queer folding doors and down a step.

An old-fashioned London tradesman, the
shopkeeper, in tie-wig and square-cut
brown coat, Mr. Goodenough, silk-merchant, received the officer with a courtly
old-world bow, and waited upon him with

the dignity of a bishop. Indeed George almost hesitated to trouble so quiet and gentlemanlike a person to show him his wares.

"I will leave it to your judgment," said George, "to select the very best and thickest silk you have among your merchandise."

The London tradesman bowed, and proceeded to lay before his customer what he pledged himself to be the very finest piece of silk in the market.

While George stood by the counter, a little child, a boy, with a wooden sword in his belt, came toddling into the shop from a doorway at the back, and stood wrapped in silent admiration of the young Major's uniform.

George turning round, and seeing the little fellow, was suddenly conscious of a new interest in children. This little one·

had large wondering eyes and curly hair, and was a sturdy, well-built infant.

"Well," he said, looking down at the child, "what is your name, eh?"

"Dorge," said the boy.

"George, if you please, General," interposed Mr. Goodenough, silk-merchant, from the counter.

"Dorge, peese, Deneral," said the child.

"I am not a General," said the Major, "but I am a George, and so you and I must be friends."

"It is an honest, worthy name, an I may make so bold," said the merchant.

"Yes," said the Major, smiling, "it should be a good name in England, when we share it with the King, eh, little George?"

"God save His Majesty!" said the tradesman, sorrowfully.

"Amen!" responded George. Turning again to the child, "are you George the First, or are there several of you?"

"The only one," said Mr. Goodenough, who had become quite talkative, from the moment the child had put in an appearance.

"George the First, eh?"

"Iss, peese, Deneral," said the boy, looking round for approval at the old gentleman, who was tying up a parcel of silk.

"Well, you are a fine little fellow," said the officer, "your eyes are as blue as a Spanish sky. Can you draw your sword?"

The child looked at the weapon that hung by the Major's side and shook his head.

"Oh, don't mind mine; it is an old one. Now then! Heads up, draw swords!"

The frank boyishness of the officer's manner captivated the child at once. He

lifted up his curly head and drew his
sword.

"Well done! Very smart! You are a
dragoon, eh?"

"Iss, peese, Deneral," said the child,
looking round at Mr. Goodenough.

"Good boy!" said the merchant, smiling.

"How old are you, little one?" asked
the Major.

The boy shook his head.

"Say four and a half, Georgy," prompted
the merchant.

"Four half, peese, Deneral," said the
boy.

"The age of *my* child," thought George,
and he sighed, as he sat down upon a
bale of goods and contemplated the bright
cheerful little face.

"Come closer, then, and let us talk; I
like you," said the officer, struggling a
little with his feelings as he thought

VOL. III.   G

of that frock and the two little empty shoes he had seen the day before.

The child walked up to the officer and laid its chubby hand in the great one that was held out to him.

"Who curls your hair?"

"Mamma."

"Why, it would do for gold lace. Shall I have a lock of it?"

"No, peese, Deneral," said the boy, putting his little hands upon his head.

"Very well, then it shall give me a kiss, will it?"

"Iss, peese, Deneral," answered the little one again, looking round for the approving nod of the merchant.

"Good boy!" said the tradesman.

The Major lifted the child up to his lips, and, kissing it, set it down upon his knee.

"A very fine little fellow, wonderful

eyes!" said George, in an aside to the mercer, while the little one was playing with the tassel of his sword.

"Yes, truly," said the mercer.

"Your grandchild, I suppose?"

"No, Major, not any relation."

"Indeed?"

"But we are as fond of the child as if it were our own. My good wife had only one, and we lost it in its infancy. We often think Providence sent us this other one to be a comfort to us in our old age. Very good of your honour to notice it."

"No, no, good of the little fellow not to be afraid of me. You adopted him, then?"

"In a manner, sir, though the child is not our own."

"Ah!" said the officer, patting the curly head and showing an inclination to hear little Dorge's history.

"It was in this way. About four years

ago, a young woman came with a child in her arms. 'Can you give me anything to do?' she said. 'I am an honest woman, anxious to work, and his father is at the wars.' Well, the sight of a child, especially if in any kind of trouble, is always too much for my good wife, who happened to be in the shop at the time; and she answers, 'Young woman, you look ill; and what sort of work do you want?' 'I am not well,' she says, 'and I can sew or keep house, or do accounts.' 'You can read and write, then?' my wife asks, and she says, 'Yes, madam, I have been well brought up, and am willing to do anything, but my child is against me getting house-work,' she says; and by this time my good wife, bless her! she had got the infant in her arms, and it was cooing up at her in its white gown and cap, and I saw the old lady had lost her heart to the child, and I

was not willing to thwart her, while my own
heart was touched by the sweet face of the
mother—an innocent, open, lovely, suffering face as you might have looked for in a
Madonna on the walls of a picture-gallery.
So Mrs. Goodenough replies, 'Well, this is
the best place you could have come to in
all London so far as the dear little child is
concerned, though I don't know that we
can really do anything for you.' 'If you
can,' says the young woman, speaking a
little outlandish, but still soft and musical
in her northern tongue, and with her innocent face streaming with tears, 'you
would never regret it.' My good dame,
still nursing and fondling the child, replies,
and very properly, that London is beset
with traps to ensnare the unwary, and how
is she to know the young woman is honest
and worthy? 'Look into my face,' she
answers, straightway, 'and into the baby's,

and you shall hear my story from first to last.' 'What have you been doing for a living?' asks my wife. 'Little or nothing as yet,' she says. 'I had a trifle of money when I came to town, and I did get a little needlework at my lodgings, but I've had no more, and my money's all gone, and what shall I do?—what shall I do?' With that my good wife she takes her into the house, and they have a long confab, and from that day to this mother and child have lived with us and proved a blessing, which is quite in keeping with the saying that in a stranger you may be entertaining an angel unawares."

"Very true," said the Major, "it is not the rule, though, that a kind action receives such prompt reward."

"No, truly; yet Providence has its own good way of ordering things. I shall send the parcel, then, to the hotel?"

" Yes, and thank you," said the Major,
lifting the child upon the counter.

"Say thank *you*, sir," said the mercer.

" Tank you, peese, Deneral," said the
child, its great blue eyes fixed on the
Major's.

" Hold out your hand," said the Major.

The child put forward its right arm, and
opened its little fat fingers.

" There's a guinea for you. Tell your
mother and this good gentleman's wife that
one of King George's officers gave it you,
because you were not afraid of him, and
because your name is George."

"Iss, peese, Deneral."

" King George, God save him ! He's
the First, do you see ?"

" Iss, peese, Deneral."

" Major George, a forlorn soldier ! He's
the Second, do you see ?"

" Iss, peese, Deneral."

"And little George with the curly hair and blue eyes! He's the Third, do you understand? And it's the Third that gets the guinea, is it not?"

"Iss, peese, Deneral."

"And what is written on the guinea? George III., you see. Well, good-bye! If I don't go, your grandfather, that Providence sent you, will think I am a child myself. But Mr. Goodenough must let me come and see you again."

"You honour us very much," replied the merchant.

"Then let it be *au revoir*, not good-bye," said George.

As he was leaving the shop, his attention was arrested by a clear, ringing voice calling "Georgey! Where are you, Georgey?"

It seemed a strangely familiar voice. It thrilled him. It set his heart beating wildly.

"Oh, I beg pardon, I thought there was nobody here but yourself, sir," said the voice, now in the shop itself.

The Major turned round.

"Merciful heaven!" he gasped. "Jessie, Jessie!"

He flung back his cloak, and opened his arms.

"George!" she exclaimed, running straight into them, to the consternation of the merchant and his wife, who now appeared upon the scene, and to the evident delight of the child, which dropped its guinea to clasp its little hands and shout, "mamma! mamma! and good denleman!"

"Oh, George!" said Jessie, smiling through her tears, "my dear, dear George! You'll never leave me again, will ye?"

"Never!" he said, and he meant it, "if you can forgive me what is past."

"Forgive ye!" said the generous woman.

"I have nothing to forgive ye! Nay, I was most to blame myself; and I'd never have pined one bit about it if they had not persecuted me down there in that cruel town. I was forced to leave it, and there was none of them, I grieve to say it, George, worse than my own father."

"My poor lassie, you've had a hard time."

"Nay, do not say so; I soon found a new father in yonder good gentleman, and more than a mother in the mistress here; and little George, bless him! I always told him his bonnie father would ride him on his knee some day. Eh, but, George, it sometimes made me sick to think ye might forget me, after all!"

"And I think I was in the mind to do so, Jessie, when I went away; but the farther I travelled from you, the more my heart seemed to go out after you, Jessie,

and though I was never much given to
praying, I have prayed many a night,
Jessie, that you might be the first woman
I should meet again in dear Old England."

The merchant and his wife were talking
together at the back of the shop, the good
tradesman telling his amiable partner how
the officer had come in about some silk
and how they had fallen to talking of the
child.

"And now, sir," said the Major, taking
the little one in his arms, "I told you I
was no general, though I am your name-
sake, you sweet little rascal! And you
must not call me General any more, but
Father !"

George's voice trembled with emotion as
he uttered the sacred name; but he quickly
overcame any outward show of excessive
sensibility.

"A plague on me," he exclaimed, "for a

conceited father, but I believe if I were to confess the truth I thought you were something like I might have been myself as a lad when I praised your good looks."

The happy fellow roared with laughter at this, and kissed the boy passionately, and the lookers-on knew that he had hard matter to prevent his apparent merriment changing into a passion of tears, which in a soldier and a strong valiant young fellow of George's build would have been too painful an exhibition; therefore Goodenough and his wife laughed, and so did Jessie.

"Iss, peese, Deneral!" George went on, fondly, imitating the boy's lisp and manner, " you handsome curly-headed little villain !"

Then he stood the boy upon the shop counter and went back a few steps to look at him.

"Heads up!" he said, and little George lifted up his head and smiled. "Draw swords!"

The child drew his wooden sabre, and George took him into his arms again, and then handed him over to his mother, down whose cheeks happy tears of joy were flowing, her lips and eyes smiling all the time, like the sun and sky during an April shower.

Here a customer entered the shop, and Mrs. Goodenough, in a matronly cap and gown, beckoned Jessie to go into the house, which Jessie did, followed by George.

"Sit down, sir, pray," said Mrs. Goodenough, "and make yourself at home here. I will leave you, that you may talk together; you will have much to say to each other."

"Nay, madam, do not let me drive you away," said George—"you to whom I owe so much gratitude for your care of my wife and child."

"Your wife!" said the old lady, somewhat reproachfully.

"In the sight of heaven, yes!" said George, "and in the sight of man too, as soon as may be!"

"Ah! then," answered Mrs. Goodenough, "Jessie, it seems, was right to trust you. I know all, sir, but I never looked to this fulfilment of her hopes."

"Then you did me wrong," said George.

"Truly, so it would appear, and I crave your forgiveness; and do not think me unkind when I say your return promises to put an end to almost the happiest period of my life. It will be a day of suffering and sorrow that sees me separated from that dear child and his mother."

"Madam, your kindness to them is a debt I owe you which I can never repay.

My wife shall not live far from you, and you shall be as free to come and go as your love for these dear ones shall desire."

The old lady disappeared, and George sat with his arm round Jessie, her head upon his shoulder, and the boy on his knee.

" Why, Jessie, you are prettier than ever, and, though I never thought you could, of course, you have improved altogether."

" How, George ?" she asked, not disguising the pleasure his compliments gave her.

" In the first place, your eyes are brighter and your lips sweeter than when I first knew them, and yet they are six or seven years older."

" Absence makes the heart grow fonder, George, that's the reason."

" And you have given up that Scotch accent."

" Not quite."

"Well, there's only just enough left to swear by, and just enough to give new music to your voice."

"Well, and what else?"

"Will you forgive me?" he began, hesitating over his next remark.

"Anything in the world, George. I am yours; you can do or say nothing I will not forgive; I am yours, as I have ever been, body and soul, from the first."

"My darling!" exclaimed George.

"Tell me, then."

"Why, you are more like a lady than you used to be."

"Ah, then I am happy; for do you know, George, I have been trying to improve myself—trying to make myself worthier of you. The moment we read of your promotion I said to myself a Captain's wife must be a lady, and when we read that you were a Major I began to despair;

but I strove my hardest. Though she was rather hard on me, I thought of the graces of Miss Hardwick of the Hall, of my lady of the Vicarage, as we used to call Miss Manners; and I also listened to the way Mrs. Goodenough pronounced the words I said awkwardly. I read good books, and Mrs. Goodenough let me go to the clergyman's night school, and I have sung in his choir as I used to sing in that other choir, at home. Several times I have been to call on the parson's wife with little George; we have all been to the theatre to see the fine comedies played; and in everything I have done, George, I have had one thought—to make myself worthy to be the wife of a soldier and a gentleman."

"My dearest Jessie, I do not deserve so good a wife! And you never doubted me?"

" Never!"

" Then it has all been God's goodness to me, this preservation of you and your love. Jessie, I am not the George you used to know. You have made a man of me. Let me explain to you how happy I am ; you cannot understand unless I tell you what happened yesterday."

Then he told her the story of that child's frock and the little empty shoes ; and Jessie shared his sorrow over the unfortunate woman. Yet she did not realize how the thought of these dumb witnesses of man's perfidy intensified George's joy at discovering her ; for she had never once thought of suicide, confident in the truth of her love and his, sensible of her own usefulness as an industrious woman, conscious of her general rectitude, except in regard to her extravagant and unreasoning love for George Wingfield. " Thus bad begins and worse remains behind " may be the

appropriate motto to fix upon such conduct as Jessie's; but, if the exception
proves the rule, let hers be set down as
the exception, an example of the all-
conquering power of woman's love.

A few days after this meeting at the
London merchant's, the sexton of the
Chesterfield parish church waited upon
the Vicar, desiring his attendance to marry
a couple by special licence. The sexton
interested his reverence in the candidates
for the holy ceremony by saying that they
expressly wished the Vicar to marry them,
and that indeed they had come a long distance for that purpose. His reverence
explained that the time was a little inop-
portune, as he was expecting his son,
Major Wingfield, to arrive during the day,
posting from London. Nevertheless, since
they desired it, he would receive them at
the altar.

It was a fresh April day, the sun pouring into the western windows of the old church, and almost lighting up the great chandeliers. When the Vicar entered the vestry, a gentleman was standing there awaiting his arrival. It was his son.

" Father !" said George.

" My son !" exclaimed the Vicar. " Let me embrace thee !"

After the first shock of surprise was over, George said,

" When we parted I had disobeyed a command that was as generous as it was noble. I am here to fulfil it, ere I cross your threshold again."

" How, George ?"

" I have found Jessie Burns, not only living in honour and repute, as you hoped and believed, but worthy by her education and graces of manner to be a gentleman's wife, and, by reason of her devotion and love, far too good to be mine."

"You amaze me!"

"Will you marry us?"

"What I said I would do five years ago, that will I do now," said the Vicar.

"Nay, then, father, I will not present her formally to you until you have made her my wife."

When the Vicar in his robes appeared at the altar, there knelt by the rails a sweet tearful young woman, attired in a modest, unpretentious way. George raised her up as the Vicar repeated the words, "Dearly beloved, we are gathered here in the sight of God."

It was a fair and goodly sight that met the Vicar's eye. A beautiful face half hidden behind a gauzy veil; a figure of graceful mould, and rich in gentle curves; dressed in a pale grey silken gown, with short waist and lace pillorine (a present from Mrs.

Goodenough); high-heeled satin shoes and white silk daintily-clocked stockings; a white Leghorn hat, tied under the chin with grey silk ribbon, and a bunch of lilacs in front of the bow; another nosegay on the left shoulder of her dress; from her right arm, suspended by a white silk cord and silver rings, a grey silk bag; the dress made rather short, the rich lace frills of the petticoat peeping out from above the curving instep of her pretty foot.

Two strangers, who rose from a seat near the altar as the Vicar entered, had no eyes except for this pretty creature, for whom they entertained even more than a parental love and admiration. They were an elderly couple, and the Vicar glanced at them as they reverently opened their prayer books to follow and take part in the cheerful service.

The ceremony was gone through with

unusual impressiveness. At the close George presented the bride to the Vicar, who kissed her, and called her his child. In the vestry, Mr. and Mrs. Goodenough came to sign the register, and to be introduced to George's father as the guardian angels who had watched over his wife and child. The Vicar was as full of joy as the young people. A messenger was sent to the Vicarage to prepare the way for the good news, while George and Jessie and the Goodenoughs returned to the Angel, where they had left the boy in charge of Mrs. Goodenough's servant, for the house and shop in London had been entrusted for a fortnight to the management of Mr. Goodenough's brother, that the dear old couple might witness the completion of Jessie's happiness, a matter on which George had insisted. They had posted from London, with Major Wingfield, Jessie, and little George.

There was joy in the ancient Vicarage house of Chesterfield.

"And all through you, mother!" said George. "If I had not thought of you, dear, at the right moment, and gone into that good merchant's house to buy you this silk gown, I might perhaps never have had the happiness to present to you this devoted daughter and grandson, and these good friends."

Jessie was a good deal abashed at first, but she held herself through the trying ordeal with exceeding grace and dignity. And, as I said before, there was joy in the Vicarage house of Chesterfield.

CHAPTER III.

THE SEQUEL TO A CERTAIN MEETING OVER AGAINST TEMPLE BAR.

"It would be believed," said the philosopher, bending low before the young Prince, who had been much overcome at the story the King's poet had chaunted so touchingly, "were it writ in the books of history, and none would cavil; but set forth in fable or the poet's song, though the slave doth build upon the sacred ground of historic lore, the mind, vain of its wit, doth itself invent doubts and questions; yet for this same romance will I relate unto thee, O Prince, the following more surprising and yet more wonderful thing that did truly happen when Four did reign in India."

From the Persian.

SIX months have elapsed since the progress of our history received the most

common-place of all history's landmarks
and halting-places, the red and black dates
of marriages and deaths. The bells that
played a muffled peal for Lord Ellerbie,
and rang joyously for George Wingfield,
as soon as the ringers discovered him, have
been called into requisition for Mary Kirk.
Though she was married in the pretty little
church at Grassmoor, she insisted upon
having the bells rung at Chesterfield; and
rung they were, right merrily.   Sergeant-
Major Bertram had hunted up Captain
North, and found him surrounded with
mechanical designs and models at Derby,
where he possessed full powers over a
mill, on the river outside the town, which
was being fitted with his machinery as fast
as he could get it made. But for the relief of this occupation, Oliver had declared
he should have gone mad. Coming to Grassmoor, however, to be best man to Bertram,

he had found another and a more delightful relief in the smiles of the Countess of
Ellerbie, who, albeit she filled her high
station with a dignity and impressiveness
that had excited the admiration of the
county, still maintained a familiar associa-
tion with those she had known previous
to her elevation. This pleasant unosten-
tation became her even better than her
coronet, behind which her father, Mr.
Hardwick, assumed grand and pretentious
airs. We shall pick up, from the conversation of certain well-known persons, during
the course of this and following chapters,
the leading incidents which have trans-
pired during the interval already mentioned,
and at the same time gather up some scat-
tered threads of our history, which at length
begins to enter the fourth quarter of its
moon.

It is the 25th of September, on which

day, authorised by Royal Charter granted
in the reign of Charles I., is held the
annual pleasure fair of Chesterfield—September 25th, 1819, the year which saw the
birth of the best and greatest monarch
that ever reigned in England, the year
before the death of one of our most weak,
misguided, and unhappy kings ; and, to
come down from the sublime to the ridi-
culous, the year in which Chesterfield was
so much exercised about the continued
crookedness of the church steeple that a
great meeting was held, to consider
whether the spire should be pulled
down.   The decision not to give it an
additional twist that should land it, leaden
chanticleer and all, in the churchyard,
seems to have inspired confidence, for soon
afterwards they removed the old bells that
had interpreted the local joy and sorrow
for many a mouldy year, and raised in

their place a new peal of ten, heavier and more dangerous to the spire's balance than the former machinery.

Sixty years ago, so near to us to-day, and yet so far off! In this little typical English borough, the second town of Derbyshire, sixty years ago they had no lucifer matches, no gas, no railways, no umbrellas, no policemen, no decent pavements. London itself was little better off, but London had within its intense organism the spirit of progress; London moved onwards hour by hour, day by day, while the somnolent Derbyshire town stood still —nay, if it moved at all, went backwards; so that to all intents and purposes, except that the oldest inhabitant still remembers the time, September 25th, 1819 might just as well have been half a century earlier, so far as the manners and customs of the people were concerned. The hiring and pleasure fairs of Chesterfield, Derby, Nottingham, Sheffield, Lincoln, at the period of our story were so many Bartlemy fairs in their way; just as mad and merry, just as strange, and noisy, and old-fashioned. They maintained, however, a certain amount of local credit and decency on account of the attendance of the upper as well as the middle classes of the district, and also because of the valuable merchandise of Yorkshire cloths, cheese, and other stores in addition to cattle and stock, which were brought to the market. Onions also, as in the old fairs of Normandy, were a great feature at this ancient fair of the autumn.

The September Fair in the old market-place is at its height of noise and bustle. Ballad-singers are chanting their ditties of love and war. The Tom Thumb of the period is ringing his bell out of the third story window of his little house. The play-actors are dancing a measure on the platform outside Richardson's Temple of the Drama. Learned pigs are telling the fortunes of Strephon and Chloe. Here is the juggler, with his flying daggers and his wondrous golden balls, plying his business on a small square of carpet to admiring crowds. The Blondin of sixty years ago is giving a tantalising example, in front of the Royal Circus, of the daring feats that await the happy throng that is paying its pennies and its twopences at the canvas doorway. There are shows without end, with vast frontages of painted canvas, on which surely are depicted far more than the seven wonders of the world—two-headed sheep, fat ladies, giants with tall men walking under their arms, lions in the grip of boa-constrictors, battle-scenes in which the French are struggling gallantly, but vainly, in spite of their superior numbers, against

British dragoons; they are all attended
with music of every description, if cym-
bals, drums, speaking-trumpets, trombones,
harps, and brass bands, all playing against
each other, can by any stretch of terms or
imagination be called music.

There are avenues of canvased stalls,
semi-tents, canvas huts, crowded with
every conceivable article of commerce;
from broad cloth to ribbons; from ribbons to brooches; from brooches to wood-
en trumpets; from piggins and sieves to
flint and tinder-box; from clocks to mouse-
traps; together with all kinds of cutlery,
both useful and ornamental, razors, knives,
daggers, gingerbread in bags, gingerbread
in squares, gingerbread thin, thick, wafery,
wedgy, gingerbread in every shape, toffy in
long sticks, raisins, nuts, apples, pears,
wafers, sealing wax, dolls. Never were
seen such red-cheeked, square-headed,

square-toed dolls, dressed and undressed.
Remedies for every ailment flesh is heir to
are offered to the wondering crowd—pills
that are magical, drops that make the old
young again and the young more beautiful
than Venus or Apollo. What a hum and
buzz it is !—children shouting, women
laughing, gongs beating, trumpets sound-
ing ; and here and there, above all, the gar-
rulous chatter of " Cheap Jack," whose
rough witticisms are sharper than his
carving knives, and whose anecdotes are
more amusing than the droll and merry
songs which he throws in, with a new
candlestick, a toasting-fork, and a broom
that will sweep cobwebs out of your mind
as well as your cellar, and half a dozen
other useful articles " for the low sum of
neither ten, nine, eight, seven, six, five,
four, nor three, but two and six—half a
crown buys the lot again, buy it who may,

for I couldn't sell them at the price unless
I stole them, and the robbery is my own
affair if it is ever found out, and the gainer
is the lucky person who has the wit to
know a bargain when he sees it. What,
not take the lot at two and six! Well,
come, I shall make the lot complete with
a gimlet that would let daylight into the
darkest prospect in life, and a hammer
with which you may drive nails into your
own coffin, if you let this chance of fur-
nishing your house for half a crown slip
by like good fortune for ever—but you
shall not, for I am simply here to amuse
myself to-day. September twenty-five is
my birthday; I always clear out my cart
on this one day in the year, whether I lose
ten pounds or ten hundred, and I live on
the losses till September comes again.
Now, here you are, going at—what do you
think? Hush! don't let anyone hear—two

shillings; that's your time of day; sold again and got the money !"

The tradesmen round the market-place are standing in their doorways, while their wives and families are at the fair. In the principal avenues of stalls opposite the Sessions House, and near the Angel, Nannie Lomas has a small canvas store, where she sells herbs and toffy and stockings which she has knitted herself; and she has many patrons, especially for the herbs, which she declares have helped to keep her alive and make her the strongest and healthiest of all the old women in Chesterfield. Many of the smaller shopkeepers of the town have also stalls in the market, the cloth and woollen dealers especially competing in the fair with the travelling merchants from other districts.

Among the distinguished visitors whose coaches and carriages drove into Chester-

field during the earlier part of the day
were the Countess of Ellerbie and Mr.
William Hardwick. Mr. Sergeant-Major
Bertram, who had taken that little farm in
the valley near Grassmoor, rode into the
town by the side of his father-in-law's car,
in which Mrs. Kirk and her daughter,
Tom's pretty wife, sat with honest Farmer
Kirk.

They all met in the fair, and made
purchases; and the Countess called at the
Vicarage, where she had already met Major
and Mrs. Major Wingfield, who had come
down from London on a short visit.
George could not forgive Chesterfield for
its cruel treatment of his wife in the days
of her trouble, and moreover he liked her
to be near her friends—the London silk-
merchant and Mrs. Goodenough. The
Countess had insisted on Mrs. Bertram
accompanying her to the Vicarage, and

the two women were delighted with little George. Probably the Countess knew at what hour Captain North would be at the Vicarage ; for he had told her he should call and see his comrade. They found him there, and he knew, when he looked into Susan's eyes, that she had not come only to see the two Mrs. Wingfields. Oliver, though he had settled down to his great work at Derby (where he was perfecting that last idea which he conceived the night before Vitoria), came to Chesterfield and the Home Farm and its neighbouring homestead of Tom Bertram nearly every week; and he never returned without spending some happy hours with his old love, the Countess of Ellerbie. For her sake he had forgiven old Hardwick his treachery, and that high and mighty pretender to family pride and honour generally contrived to keep out of North's way as much as possible. Susan had a hand in this, and she found it less difficult to forgive him than North did, not simply because he was her father, but from the change which his perfidy had brought in her fortune. She found a wonderful comfort in having, for the first time in her life, as much money as she could desire; in possessing an assured position of precedence and wealth; and she would not deny, when communing with herself, that a title is a pleasant distinction, and that there is a peculiar fascination about diamonds, and an especial delight in being mistress of a grand old house and a fine estate. Not that these things would have weighed with her against the love of Oliver North. Nor would she have accepted them at the price of the awful death of her infatuated husband of an hour. His miserable end had preyed upon her mind for months; but

Cupid or the devil often in her misery
suggested to her that good fortune had
struck the blow in the interest of Oliver
North. It was these promptings of her
woman's heart that made her seek consolation in the chapel of Father Busby;
for there were pangs of remorse in her
sense of the daily growth of her old
love for Oliver North. Father Busby
was a shrewd man as well as a discreet
priest. He encouraged the Countess to
feel that the hand of Providence had not
been absent from the events which had
saved her from the embraces of a man who
had literally bought her from her father,
and in whose love there was not the divine
spirit which should burn on the altar of
holy matrimony. Nevertheless, let it not
be thought that Father Busby was only a
time-serving priest. He had conceived a
sincere respect and fatherly affection for

the young Countess. He recognized in her conduct a deep sense of duty, and a devotion to the possible wishes and desires of her dead lord, which showed her to be a high-minded woman, and one quite worthy of rank and riches.

It was late in the afternoon, when the Countess and the Kirks and the visitors from the outlying districts of Chesterfield had gone home, that a swaggering, ragged, and yet distinguished-looking man came along the principal avenue of the fair, walking with a showy cane and waving people out of his path. A curious figure, a sort of aristocratic gipsy; a tall man with black hair, well-marked eyebrows, and a dark, sallow face slightly pitted with the small-pox, which had sharpened his features and given his face an eager, bird-of-prey look which might have suggested the countenance of Mephistopheles. He wore a moustache and imperial. His attire was travel-stained. He carried a sword, and over his foreign-like garb he wore a cloak that was tattered and torn.

"By mi Leddy!" exclaimed Nannie Lomas, "here's a gentleman as fine as a peacock, and yet as ragged as a badger after a baiting!"

"Ah!" said Dick Holmes, who had been drinking at the Angel, "he looks like a gipsy king on the loose."

"Well, old hag, and what do you sell?" asked the stranger, standing before Nannie Lomas's modest store with an insolent air, as he observed the adjacent stall-keepers staring at him.

"Nothing that's useful to you," replied Nannie; "they sell thread and needles farther on."

"Oh, don't you love me because I make my own ribbons?" he rejoined, laughing.

"Ribbons! I reckon sort o' ribbons you want is a halter," said Nannie.

"Indeed, say you so? Well, it's some hundreds of years since you stood at the altar, and the poor man didn't long survive, eh?" rejoined the stranger, passing on, the crowd that began following him laughing at his retort.

"Ah, you cowards!" exclaimed Nannie, "why don't you leather him? You would if you'd a ha'porth o' courage among lot on ye!"

"Well, and what have you to sell since you lost your beauty?" asked the impudent stranger, pausing before another respectable dame's store, as if his object was to foment a broil.

"Why, my son, if he was such a scarecrow as you!" screamed the dame, one Sally Warner, locally famous for her sharp tongue and fresh fish.

"Ho! ho! Ah! ah!" roared the crowd.
"Well done, missus!"

"You've no need for a scarecrow now,"
answered the ragged gentleman, nothing
abashed; "*your* harvest has been gathered."

"Good! ah, ha!" laughed Dick Holmes,
coming on the scene, "one to the vagabond! At him again, missus!"

"Nay, let him be, he's on's way to th'
rag-shop, donna stop him."

"That's one for his nob," remarked one
of the crowd, amidst another laugh, as the
stranger walked on up the avenue, pausing,
however, at another stall, presided over by
a dark, attractive girl, who looked out at
her customer from a framework of drapery
consisting of yellow and red handkerchiefs,
mittens, comforters, chintz, and laces of
all kinds.

"What will this cost me, little hop-o-my-thumb?" he asked, raising a handkerchief upon the end of his stick, and waving it like a flag.

"A broken head, if you insult my daughter!" answered a rough-looking fellow, confronting him.

"Hurrah!" shouted the crowd. "Billy Nipper's walking up to him! Billy's the weight for him!"

"A broken head!" said the stranger, mocking his new antagonist; "and who'll give it me?"

"Why, me!"

"You! What! Have you forgotten the cudgelling I gave you at Grassmoor?"

"You!"

"Yes! It may be six years ago; but I told you, you should not forget it as long as you lived!"

Billy stepped back, and the crowd listened. Several local tradesmen had pushed their way into the ring of people that hemmed the stranger in, he towering above them, with his slouch hat and his dark, uncanny face.

"You cudgelled me!" said Billy.

"Yes, don't you know me, now I am so well dressed?"

"Know thee! why, who art thou?"

Billy paused, and looked round at his neighbours to make sure that the mysterious stranger, ghost, goblin, or reality, could take no sudden and undue advantage of him.

"Look at me! How's my little child, your daughter's sister?"

"Curse you!" said Billy Nipper, turning pale; "you are not Scruton?"

"You are a liar, I am!" answered the villain.

Billy, with an oath, raised his stick and rushed at him; but Philip Scruton disarmed him with ease, and tossed the poor villager's weapon among the crowd.

"Scruton!" said Dick Holmes; "why, he was killed long ago!"

"Was he!" rejoined the returned heir.

"Why, I've read thy epitaph on thy tombstone!"

"Then you've read a lie. But there! It is not good manners to come to the fair and buy nothing; I must patronise the old town."

He strode up to a dealer in clothes, who turned upon him promptly.

"If you are Scruton, you scamp, pay for what you've had already."

"How?"

"Pay the creditors you ran away from."

"I'll pay you with my cane," Scruton answered.

"Hear the villain!" exclaimed Billy

Nipper, who had recovered his stick and with it some of his courage; "will you hear him insulting everybody? Let's chuck him out o' the fair!"

Billy's sudden display of valour was infectious. A dozen bystanders, following his lead, rushed at Scruton, who stepped aside, flung back his cloak, and drew his sword.

"Stand off! I'll make the man who advances as ragged as my doublet!"

The assailants fell back before the glittering steel as Mr. Septimus Dobbs (who had just left the Angel, and had walked up to see what the commotion might mean) appeared in the rear of Scruton.

"Are you all cowards?" screamed Sally Warner, seizing a wooden mallet and flinging it with all her might at Scruton, who, ducking his head, allowed the awkward missile to land in the bosom of Mr. Septimus Dobbs, who felt the breath suddenly knocked out of his miserable body.

The crowd went into fits of laughter as Dobbs was seen to go down under the fishermonger's mallet, and Scruton, sheathing his sword, joined in the merriment.

While the lookers-on were laughing, Dobbs scrambled upon his feet, rubbed his chest, felt at his legs, and finally, discovering that no bones were broken, picked up the mallet and began to bluster.

"Whose property is this?" he asked. "I won't ask who flung it, because I don't want any person to criminate himself or herself, as the case may be."

"It's my property, and I banged it at the head of that villain Scruton," shouted Sally Warner; "an' you can mak' the morst on it, criminate or no!"

"Well done, Sally!" exclaimed Dick Holmes, amidst a loud cheer.

"What!" said Dobbs, starting back and dropping the mallet, "who did you say? Mr. Scruton—the Honourable Philip Scruton?"

"Yes," said Scruton; "very much at your service, Mr. Dobbs; and I wish I was so fortunate as to have you at mine, for I seem likely to want some one to defend me from my old friends."

The crowd had grown into quite considerable numbers by this time, several of the minor shopkeepers of the town having put in an appearance.

"At *your* service!" exclaimed Dobbs, taking off his hat, and bending low; "it would be an honour. Defend you from your friends! What offence could they offer?"

"They seem troubled about some old debts," said Scruton.

VOL. III.   K

"Yes," said Billy Nipper; "he not only robbed us of our money and worse, but he has given it out as he's dead, and now he comes back and insults us."

"Oh, no, no!" said Dobbs, reprovingly, to the speaker and the crowd generally; "you don't know what you are saying; you don't know to whom you are talking." And then, turning to Scruton, he said, "Your Grace must forgive them. I am sure they are as glad to see you as I am."

The crowd began to talk among themselves, seeing this display of humility on the part of Dobbs, who, as a rule, was an overbearing man, and not likely to bend where thrift did not follow fawning.

"We all thought you dead," went on Dobbs; "we mourned you dead, and grieved over our loss."

"And I had been dead but for this good sword!" said Scruton, patting the handle of his weapon; "I was captured by bandits and held at first for ransom, and then for other reasons—reasons of State."

"Bandits!" exclaimed several of the crowd, who were now all eyes and ears.

"Forced to live in caves and rocky passes, in ruins and catacombs, literally in tombs, a prisoner, a slave," said Scruton, addressing himself to Dobbs, but speaking loudly that all might hear.

"The Lord preserve us!" exclaimed Dobbs.

"Not a penny would my unnatural uncle part with. But the day came when I could strike a blow for freedom. I did it, and here I am."

"A plucky devil after all!" said Dick Holmes. "I always heard he was."

"Fought my way to a Spanish port, was protected, treated well, got over to England in a trading ship, and have walked

K 2

from Dover to Chesterfield. Walked !
Think of it, Master Dobbs ! Walked ! For
I couldn't afford to ride. And because I
am a little merry at getting back again,
because it is Fair day, and I feel like wearing the cap and bells—gad's life ! they set
on me like curs on a stranger dog."

The crowd began to feel a little sorry
for Scruton, and ashamed of their in-
hospitality.

"But you will forgive them, your Grace,"
said Dobbs.

"Your Grace !" repeated Scruton, "what
do you mean ?"

"Gentlemen, neighbours, townsmen, and
friends," shouted Dobbs, "welcome the lost
heir ! The new Earl of Ellerbie will pay
you all he owes, and with interest. Three
cheers for the Right Honourable the Earl
of Ellerbie, and master of Brackenbury
Towers !"

Dobbs raised his hat, and the crowd shouted " Hurrah !"

" What is the meaning of this ?" asked Scruton, looking round with real or well-acted amazement. " It is true I am Lord Ellerbie's heir, but that is nothing new to you. I have no reason to respect him, nor have you ; for it would seem, from your grievance about my old debts, that he did not pay them—let me pack off to fight for King and country, and never paid a stiver —not even, it seems, when he thought me dead."

" Hush ! gentlemen," said Dobbs, raising his finger impressively, " he does not know what has happened."

" What *has* happened, then ?" asked Scruton.

" My lord, my lord !" said Dobbs, " your uncle died nearly a year ago. Brackenbury Towers is waiting for its rightful owner.

Chesterfield welcomes home again the lost heir. Again I ask you, neighbours, to give the returned exile, the gallant Ellerbie, three cheers!"

The crowd cheered lustily. Scruton bowed his head sorrowfully for a minute, and then, waving his hand for silence, said,

" A year ago ! You have done your funeral honours, then, to my uncle; and I cannot expect you to weep afresh."

Dick Holmes and some of the other lookers-on sniggered at this remark, detecting in Scruton's tone and manner the cynicism which the new lord felt.

" I am necessarily a little shocked, as we all must be at the first news of a friend or relative's death, even if he has not behaved exactly well to us. But I do not expect you to humour this little natural weakness in me. I thank you for your reception of the returned exile; and I invite you one and all to what good cheer the Angel may afford. Come, gentlemen, *tenants* I may perhaps rightly say, for the Ellerbie property represents a big rent-roll in Chesterfield! Mr. Dobbs will preside over your wants. Come, and let us drink to our better friendship! I will show you how the Lords of Ellerbie used to treat their friends in the good old merry days of our fathers."

Scruton thereupon took the arm of Lawyer Dobbs. The crowd cheered and made way for them, forming in procession in the rear, and marching in a body to the Angel.

Pausing under the piazzas, and on the threshold of the well-known hostelry, Scruton turned round and said,

"Mr. Septimus Dobbs, you are my lawyer and steward, as you were my late revered uncle's; order what you think I require, in my present condition, and of what tradesmen you choose; but first set the Angel taps running till all these dear friends I see around me have drunk their fill."

"Hurrah! hurrah!" shouted the crowd, pressing into the Angel yard, where they were presently regaled to their hearts' content, and to the increasing confusion of the fair.

On no 25th of September, past or present, were so many drunken men and women seen and heard reeling and howling about the streets. It was absurd for the parish constables to attempt to grapple with the novel situation; and so they quietly looked on.

In the meantime, Dobbs and Scruton,

closely tiled and carefully ensconced in the lawyer's dining-room, held a council of war.

CHAPTER IV.

THE PLOT THICKENS : AND IT SURPRISES

LAWYER DOBBS.

It will have blood; they say, blood will have blood :
Stones have been known to move, and trees to speak ;
Augurs and understood relations have
By magot-pies, and choughs, and rooks, brought forth
The secret'st man of blood.

SHAKSPERE.

THERE was a calm severity in the general appearance of Mr. Dobbs's dining-room ; and yet in the aspect of the apartment there was a kind of mystery, a sort of perpetual wink of self-conscious-ness, a suggestion in both chairs and tables and oaken cabinets of " we are not so simple as we look; mind you don't criminate yourself, or it will be the worse for you."

The apartment was positively grim in its simplicity; yet Dobbs brought out from a spirit-case a bottle of brandy that was as old and as delightful as if some privileged prince had invoked the liquor. Scruton smacked his lips at it.

" That is the drink to keep a man up to his work," he said.

" And so your lordship's steward thought when he placed it before you," said Dobbs.

" Now observe, Dobbs, drop the lordship for the present; let us talk as equals, for our alliance is cemented by deeds that bind us more strongly than mere stewardship."

" Referring to the papers you signed in London, in which you were generous enough to assign to me certain properties, including the mortgages on Hardwick's mill and the Hall?" asked Dobbs, helping himself.

"Referring to our partnership generally, our alliance against Fate, our forced drafts on Fortune."

"Yes," answered Dobbs, offering his snuff-box to Scruton, of which Scruton took no notice, and upon which Dobbs took a deep reflective pinch.

"Now tell me all about the—the death of Lord Ellerbie, the murder, or whatever it was called."

"Tell you? For what purpose?"

"For my information."

"Are you serious?"

"Yes, I know nothing."

"Know nothing?"

"From the time the affair was discovered, no."

"Up to the death of the old Earl you are posted?"

"Yes."

"Nay, then 'twere best you tell me what has happened to you since."

"Did it surprise you that I made no sign?"

"Yes and no. I had not given you credit for so much patience and discretion."

"You were right as to patience, wrong as to discretion; no professional spy, no missionary of a secret society, could out-match me in discretion."

"Say you so?"

"Ay! you do not know me, Dobbs."

"'Tis not my own fault; you leave my knowledge dependent on my own speculations."

"You thought that story of my arrival at Dover and my walk here a lie?"

"Not exactly a lie."

"It was true; I came here from Spain, in a merchant-ship to Dover, thence on foot and with the aid of such lifts by the way as I could get; and they were not many, for the knaves in charge of cart and carriage would not trust me too near their vile persons."

"You surprise me."

"I was laid up with small-pox in Madrid."

"You carry the ravages of the disorder . in your face."

"Do I, you old fox?—yet you have not inquired how it fared with me, penniless as you must know I have been."

"Nay, my lord, 'twas not my fault; I did both write to London and go to London in quest of you."

"Is that a truth?"

"It is, most assuredly."

"Then I forgive you, Monsieur Reynard."

"A truce to calling names, and waste of time; how came you at Madrid?"

"Know, then, my reverend friend, that there be affairs of moment in this life when 'tis advisable to be in two places at one time. Six months ago I was in Spain, partly in my own interest, partly by command of an Order to which I belong, partly that I might return and leave public trace of my return to England, and to Chesterfield, to hear how it has fared with thee, good, patient Dobbs, like a general who is anxious to hear the result of the operations of a stout ally in a united campaign, and to reap the reward of courage, discretion, and skill."

"You are more vague in what you impart than is your wont."

"Am I so? Then let me drink; this goodly liquor will clear my brain."

While Scruton filled his glass, Dobbs

stirred the fire and furtively emptied his tumbler into the ashes. He meant to keep cool, and yet to appear free and open in his remarks and conduct. Refilling his glass, he pledged his guest ostentatiously.

"Now," said Scruton; "your report! It is all a blank to me since—well, no matter; go on from the time they found Lord Ellerbie saying his last prayer by the side of his dumb ancestor, the knight in effigy."

"They held an inquest; verdict, 'Found dead.'"

"Not murder?"

"No."

"Not suicide?"

"No; they left it an open question."

"To be revived, eh?"

"By the action of the higher authorities, yes; and the matter is in the hands of the Home Office."

"Ah, what have they done?"

"Offered a reward for further evidence, and in case the death be murder a reward of one hundred pounds for such information as shall lead to the conviction of the assassin, and a free pardon to any confederate who gives up the real perpetrator of the deed."

"Yes?" said Scruton, a little impatiently, as Dobbs hesitated and looked at him in the face for the first time. "Yes, don't criminate yourself, Dobbs, or I may confess and hang you, as you hanged my indiscreet young acquaintance Marks."

The lawyer rose to his feet as if he had been stung. Scruton burst out into a fit of laughter. Dobbs went to the door and locked it, though he knew his servants were all in bed. He drew a screen across the door. He pulled the curtains tightly over the closed shutters.

"There are jests and jests," he said, coming back to the table, which had been drawn up to the hearth.

"Forgive me, Dobbs; I couldn't help it, you looked so devilish solemn; the brandy tempted me, and I did sin; I am penitent."

"To this offer of the Government I added a reward of three hundred pounds on behalf of the family," said Dobbs.

"A wise judge, a discreet ally! Go on, good Dobbs, thou art a jewel!" said Scruton.

"But for the officiousness of that pompous fool Hardwick these notifications would not have been issued. The superstitious had already put the affair down to the fulfilment of the family legend that the last of the Ellerbies should——"

"Yes, yes, go on, you interest me now. Well?" said Scruton.

"And the people in general, the authorities, too, had attributed the death to a sudden impulse of suicide, brought on by a morbid condition of mind, or what not. But Hardwick must persuade the Countess to have the old chapel razed to the earth, and thereupon is discovered a secret passage leading from the boat-house by the lake into the chapel."

" The devil !"

" Which might not have been of great importance but for the evidence of the forester, brought forward by the constable, that he saw a man with a dark lantern in the boat-house the night before the affair— the suicide, or what not—and that he rushed in when the light went out and found no one there."

" Whew ! A bold forester that !"

" A ghost, of course, was the proper conclusion to that story, for ghosts have always been popular at Brackenbury. But when Hardwick discloses this hitherto

L 2

unknown passage between the lake and the chapel, 'a murder!' exclaims the whole township—the entire county, in fact."

"That meddling old woman Hardwick was never fit to live! Curse me, if I believe he can be the father of that magnificent high and mighty wench Susan of Brackenbury, Countess of Ellerbie, by George! Damme, Dobbs, shall I marry her, break her heart, and wipe my feet on that impostor Hardwick, eh?"

Dobbs consulted his snuff-box.

"Eh—what do you say to that?"

"Mr. Oliver North is the gentleman to whom you should propound that question."

"Why, has he turned up?—is he to the fore?"

"He appeared the day of the marriage, an hour or so after the poor old bridegroom was found dead."

"Yes, well?"

"Presented himself at the wedding-feast, frightened the bride, threatened her father, would have drawn upon the guests, but was interrupted by Father Busby's appearance and announcement of Lord Ellerbie's death."

"Hold! let me think!" exclaimed Scruton, getting up, walking to the other end of the room, and sitting down again. "Your story is stronger than your brandy; I could drink a hogshead dry and not be drunk to-night. Go on, Dobbs."

"Shortly afterwards North disappeared. Some seven or eight weeks later he re-appeared, and since then he has become the accepted suitor for the hand of his former sweetheart, your uncle's widow."

"Wonder upon wonders!" exclaimed Scruton. "I am just in time, then, the good saints be thanked!"

"And I am cashiered this very day!

Truly 'twould seem as if Providence had brought you here at this juncture. Only this day, of all others in the year, one Charles Mercer, a pettifogging, litigious, designing villain, doth give me notice by the Countess's authority, written by Hardwick, signed by his daughter, to hand over my trust and my deeds to him, and I am forbidden to cross the threshold of Brackenbury Towers again."

"Thou shalt be revenged, Dobbs—thou shalt be revenged!"

"Ay, trust me! I am not of a vindictive mould, but I do hate Hardwick—that I will confess."

"No, there is no malice in thee, Dobbs," said Scruton, his moustache rising a little with the cynical smile that moved his lips, "not one iota of it; thou art full of the milk of human kindness."

"I am as heaven made me," answered Dobbs; "and I vow that——"

"You wouldn't harm a fly. True, Reynard, thy nature is gentle, thy soul a blank sheet whereon Nature has written Purity; but at last the viper has stung thee, Dobbs. The serpent thou hast warmed in thy bosom has turned on thee; and thou wilt have the thing under thy heel; and so thou shalt, and so thou shalt—we'll shake hands on that!"

Scruton put out his hand. Dobbs gripped it.

"But 'tis strange," went on Scruton, from a half-bantering tone of theeing and thouing to one of nervous earnestness, "you have not placed North's neck in jeopardy."

"How?"

"What did they discover by the side of the body?"

" Nothing in particular."

" Not a knife ?"

" Truly, yes, a knife."

" What has become of it ?"

" The coroner or the constable hath it."

"Good! How did you ask should North's neck be put into jeopardy ? He returns on the day of the murder, he disappears, he comes back, he is the accepted suitor of the Countess ?"

" Yes," said Dobbs ; " do not think all this has escaped me ; as the steward and legal adviser of the Ellerbies, I laid these facts privately before the Bow Street runner who has the matter in hand ; but on testing the theory by practice, trying the distance on horseback from Brackenbury to Chesterfield, we found that the space could not be covered in time for a man who had killed Lord Ellerbie to put in an appearance at the Hall."

"Eh? What? Was that all that stood in the way of his arrest?"

"I verily believe so. The girl at the Angel saw him leave the hotel, and the next evidence is his presence at the Hall when the death is announced by Father Busby. He could not have been in Chesterfield and at Brackenbury at one and the same time."

"A trick!" exclaimed Scruton; "a stale device—my own subterfuge, every man's that hath adventures, the first principle of a great operation in the world of intrigue and crime; 'tis the first thought of the cracksman, an *alibi*, the triumph of swift horsemanship, the trump card in the science of disguises and doubles. North killed Lord Ellerbie!"

Dobbs poked the fire, took snuff, and then swallowed his glass of brandy at a gulp.

" What evidence have you besides this theorising ?"

"The knife! His own knife! I'll swear to it!"

"You will!" exclaimed Dobbs.

"Ay, and prove it! And, what is more, bring forward at a pinch the man who was his double. Nay, more!—Put thy cursed liquor aside for a moment!"

Scruton rose from his seat, again passed his hand over his brow, stroked his chin, and, stopping suddenly before Dobbs, without sitting down, said,

"Begad, I have it! His confederate shall confess, his double shall round upon him, and get the reward and the pardon. A free pardon and three hundred pounds, did you not say?"

"Yes, that is the sum, a free pardon the temptation."

"Now pass the bottle, my good friend,

and confess yourself dull-pated," said Scruton, sitting down and re-filling his glass.

"You grasp the case with skill," said
Dobbs.

"Get me a warrant for Oliver North's
arrest."

"When?"

"To-morrow, as soon as there is a magistrate stirring."

"Before you have examined the knife
you say is his?" asked Dobbs.

"No, no; that is a point to you; you are
a sly boots, Dobbs; I recall my charge that
thou art dull-witted."

"I do not presume to match myself with
one who has seen so much of this wicked
world," said Dobbs, smiling in a ghastly
kind of way.

"Well, then, you comprehend now what
my plan is; we'll hang Oliver North! I
told him I would be even with him—so I

will. And that the fair Susan may not be disappointed again, and may still be mistress of the estates of Brackenbury, she shall still have a lord of Ellerbie for her husband. Curse me, but the bare idea of it fires my blood, and makes me chide the tardy time! To-morrow, Dobbs, to-morrow, let us take possession; to-morrow, before they have got news of our return; to-morrow, while North is hot in his love-making, and Hardwick pluming himself on your discomfiture. Shall it be so, Dobbs—shall it be so?"

"It shall, by God!" exclaimed Dobbs, losing his self-control for the first time under the magnetic influence of Scruton's sanguine picture, his own malicious hatred of Hardwick, the brandy which he had drunk, and the undoubted surprise of the new phase which the Ellerbie affair had developed.

"Well said!" was Scruton's response, "my able lieutenant, well said! Are we true to each other?"

"To death!" answered Dobbs.

"Then give reins to your wishes; you shall realize them all; ask me what you will. Consider the Hall and the factory your own. Foreclose the mortgages at once. The Potter's Fields you wanted, they are your own. The Hasland property, it is yours. The market-house and West End estate, your own. These new deeds, prepare them when you will, and let them be companions to those I signed in London. Am I generous?"

"Most generous!" exclaimed Dobbs. "I will deserve your liberality."

"You have deserved it!"

"I am honoured by your confidence and good opinion. Now, my lord, pray you pause for a moment. Let us consider.

The story of your long absence.   Is this
how it was?   You enlisted, you marched,
you were taken by bandits in Spain, you
knew nothing of the report of your death;
having quarrelled with your uncle, you
had no reason to communicate with him;
you were an exile, a wanderer on the earth,
in short; finally, you escaped, you got a
ship, you were poor, you came home."

"My history to the letter."

"Is it not odd to be taken by bandits
when we were fighting for Spain?"

"Not at all."

"But not being ransomed, would they
not kill you, or give you your liberty?"

"They made a slave of me. I was always
a cosmopolitan, always a traveller. I have
lived in all climes. The truth is, I became
a bandit, against my will, it is true; but
they discovered my talents—I spoke their
language, I liked their roving life. I

remained with them; I wanted change; I longed to see England; I got to Madrid, was stricken with small-pox; at last I am here! Put upon my oath, I will frankly admit that, if my country is ungrateful enough to do it, they may hand me over to the Spanish Government as a bandit, an outlaw, but I don't think they will do that."

"No, not they," answered Dobbs; "and the knife?"

"I can swear I saw it in North's possession when we marched together, two recruits in His Majesty's service."

"Yes," said Dobbs. "I will make a note of this while you rest; you must be tired. Shall I show you to your chamber?"

"No, show me to your larder, and while you write I'll eat."

Dobbs took up a candle; they went together to the larder, and Scruton, cutting a slice of venison, brought it on a plate to the dining-room, while Dobbs carried other things, and placed on the board a bottle of wine.

"I thought it best that the servants should retire," said Dobbs.

"By the saints, you have the head of a Solomon!" said Scruton, "and the larder of a monk!"

While Scruton ate a hearty supper, during which the clock struck an hour after midnight and the watchman in Glueman-gate proclaimed the time "and a cloudy morning," Dobbs was busy writing upon large sheets of paper.

"Beg pardon, Dobbs; did you order me a new wardrobe?"

"I commanded the Ellerbie tradesmen to bring here by six o'clock in the morning such outfit of clothes and jewellery as they might think would be required by an ill-treated heir, who had been knocked about in the world penniless, and who had come afoot ragged and hungry to find that his cruel and unnatural uncle was dead, and that fortune no longer barred him from his estates and his title."

"Most excellent Dobbs! you improve. You have been hiding your talents from me all these years, your accomplishments of wisdom and eloquence."

"The occasion makes the man," said Dobbs.

"And now some tobacco!" said Scruton, his supper finished, "to soothe my nerves, and then I will not speak again until you command me."

Dobbs went to an old cabinet which looked demure enough for a hidden library of homilies and the Fathers bound in solemn cloth; but it contained a shelf of pipes and tobacco. Scruton selected therefrom a long clay calumet, and, filling the spacious bowl with the dark, strong weed of the time, took a spill from an ecclesiastical-looking ornament that stood on the tall oak fireplace, lighted his pipe, and, stretching his legs into the firelight that flashed on the brass fender, leaned his back against the table, and thought out the programme of the next day's dangerous work.

CHAPTER V. .

SUNSHINE AND SHADOW.

"Misfortunes," answered the Arab, "should always be expected. If the eye of hostility could learn reverence or pity, excellence like yours had been exempt from injury. But the angels of affliction spread their toils alike for the virtuous and the wicked, for the mighty and the mean. Do not be disconsolate . . . . I will fix your ransom."

Rasselas.

IT was Tom Bertram who had brought Oliver North back to Susan's feet, and Oliver had been nothing loath to find a welcome in the Countess's eyes. Tom had thus returned Susan's good service to

M 2

him, and Mrs. Bertram insisted upon saying that everything had happened for the
best in Oliver's case, since he would now
have for his wife a Countess with lands
and jewels and wealth ; whereas, on the
other hand, it was well known her father
was but a poor man, though he had man-
aged to keep up appearances. Tom would
tell his wife that Oliver had a sufficient
fortune in his mechanical inventions, and
that one day he would show them wonders, which was not without a good basis ;
for Oliver had been promptly taken into
partnership by a manufacturer at Derby,
on the mere strength of a few designs and
roughly-constructed models.

Susan had felt compelled to justify herself so far as it was possible in Oliver's
eyes, and he had stared aghast at the
ribbon which that false letter had enclosed
in token of his death ; while the fraudulent

soldier, who had been introduced to Susan
by her father, also excited his ire and indignation beyond all bounds. It was plain
to both of them that they had been the
victims of a cruelly elaborate conspiracy,
and that her father had a guilty knowledge of it. He must have known of the
robbery which had been committed while
Oliver was embarking for Spain. Susan
herself acknowledged that he must, and
yet she found excuses for him in his
family pride, his want of means, his terror
of poverty, and possibly some secret financial hold the late Lord Ellerbie had over
him.

Moreover, Susan felt that she too need-
ed an apologist, and, in trying to see ex-
tenuating circumstances connected with
her father's base and indefensible conduct,
she suggested generous excuses for herself.
When Oliver knew all her story, what

could he do but forgive her, since she in those old past days forgave him when he deserted her and left her fainting in Nannie Lomas's cottage? Besides, what could he do when he found her humble—when, countess though she was, proud as he had known her even when he loved her most, she was now gentle and submissive as any village maiden? He was only too happy to take her into his arms, she glad to be there.

What a happy time it was after all! To be to Susan what he had never been before, except for those few moments when the drums were beating and the intensity of the situation had forced from her proud lips the declaration of her love. It was too sweet, too real to be a dream; for dreams soon come to an end; while here was Oliver for hours together with Susan in a palace, not only her suitor, but her

accepted suitor, and not only her accepted
suitor, but engaged to be married to her,
and only waiting for the day to be fixed.
After all his troubles, his anxieties, his
hopes, his fears, his disappointments, to
be sitting by her side at last, her hand in
his, his arm round her waist!   To be telling her of his adventures, to have had adventures worth telling, and hopes worth
cherishing!   The military authorities had
reinstated Oliver in his commission, and
had allowed him to retire and sell out, for
the spirit of invention still held him, the
old object of his early days still possessed his thoughts, during those moments
when Susan was not wholly there.   Already one of his most cherished schemes
in regard to the weaving of silk was in a
fair way for execution, the development
of those designs and patterns which had
been wiped out only for a time in the old

mill by the Hall. But Oliver's dream
went far beyond these plans. He was
laying in the lines of an automatic mill
which should practically work by itself.
It was more like a fairy tale than a serious
proposition as he told it to Susan; and it
was a secret joy to her to feel that, as
her husband, his ideas need not be crippled
for want of money; that he might make
experiments of the most expensive character without regard to mere financial con-
siderations. She had only one fear, the
turbulent character of the times, the oppo-
sition which improved machinery was meeting with all through the North of England.
Oliver told her all this would cease; that
a few reckless men would first sacrifice
themselves on the old blood-stained altar of
ignorance and superstition; that the bless-
ings of peace would intervene to intensify
and enlarge the claims of commerce to

such an extent as to give every man in England plenty of work; that in due course the jealousy excited by new inventions would die out, and the man who augmented Great Britain's power of production by breathing the breath of life, as it were, into the dream of the scientist and the mechanist, would be hailed with the plaudits of the entire nation.

Susan fairly hung upon his words, and admiration was mingled with her love. She was happy. The craving of her strong yet ill-balanced nature was satisfied in this man. She had found her master, and she had given him the right in her own estimation to be her superior. He had been true to her; she had been false to him. So she argued in her own mind, and in taking her with another's name, though it was written under a coronet, he had placed her under an obligation. She liked this sense of inferiority. Even while excusing herself she exaggerated what she called her sin against true love, comparing in fancy his everlasting devotion to her memory in the event of the report of her death instead of his. He would, she felt sure, have lived a sort of poetic widowerhood for her sake. How much more should she have gone into perpetual mourning for him? She said all this to herself, and rejoiced in this hero-worship for which her soul had craved, a hero-worship lifted into the highest ideal of perfect manhood by her love—a tender secret in those days when first Oliver likened his heart to the silken ball with which her kitten was playing in the first chapter of this romance—which now gave itself up to adoration. "Here is a man," she said, "whom success not only does not spoil, but only contributes to his

modest faith in the destiny that awaits him
as a benefactor to his race, for he said, 'I
will make a machine that shall be man's
slave, and the day will come when they
who follow me shall give to England
Aladdin's lamp and ring!' Here is a
man," she went on saying to herself, "who
steps entirely out of his walk in life, and
teaches veteran soldiers how to fight, out-
does Valour herself, and is content to come
home and have his sword beaten into an
instrument of peace, content to give up
the glory of trumpet and banner for the
calm, undemonstrative, and at present un-
appreciated victories of science; and whose
love for me was so great that he could
lay aside the ambition of his life and seek
oblivion in the uniform of a private
soldier. But Fame found him even there;
and good Fortune gives him to me." It
was in this wise that Susan depreciated

herself before the idol of her heart. It had
been her lot to discover in her own father
how weak and mean man can be; and in
her secret comparison of Oliver North with
every man she had ever met her lover
seemed a demi-god. It was refreshing to
have some one to lean upon. She, who
had looked down all her life upon others, at
last had found some one she could look up
to, a man who could guide and protect her,
a companion who interested her, the per-
fection of her young life's dream, the
realization of half-formed instincts which
had stirred her heart and soul in those
early days when she nursed her love as a
tender secret, hardly to be acknowledged
even to herself; when the vanity of youth
and the consciousness of her own beauty
prompted her to feel that she was a prize
worth winning, and sometimes that Oliver's
love, though unspoken except in the lan-

guage of the eye, was a presumption.
How all this was changed now in the
woman's passion for the man she really
loved when a girl, who had come back to
her when most he seemed to have left her
for ever!

The time had at last arrived when Oliver
was anxious that Susan should name the
day, and that the very earliest, for their
marriage. On the night of the September
Fair, sitting by the fire at Tom Bertram's
and talking the future over by the light
of Mary's experience, he had come to the
conclusion that not another day should
pass without this all-important matter
being settled. There was undoubtedly an
outward show of respect due to the dead,
and it was right that Susan should give up
a certain time to widow's weeds; but "the
living must also not be forgotten," as Mary
remarked, and Oliver thought she was a

very sensible as well as delightful little woman.

So it happened that on the 26th of September, in the yellow drawing-room at Brackenbury overlooking the terrace, Oliver North was unusually persistent in his wooing, and he had entered upon the subject of their speedy marriage at this time with a sort of prophetic sense of some threatened danger.

"Ah! if you only knew how my heart longs for that happy day!" he said.

"Not more than mine; but let me whisper the confession in your ear," she answered, and not attempting to hide the blush that mantled her cheek.

"My darling!" he exclaimed, "then let it be no longer delayed."

"If a young widow should fix her second wedding-day ere her first lord has been buried only a little more than six short

months, it would scandalize all the county,"
she said, now trying to play the woman's
part that has deference for her sex and regard to the judgment of society, though all
the time her heart only prompted her to
say, " Oliver, take me when you will, I am
thine, and it is for thee to command!"

" But do we owe anything to society, to
the county?" was Oliver's reply. " Have
we not waited long enough at others'
bidding? Has not custom, not to say
villainy, postponed our happiness too long
already?"

" Think, Oliver dear, I am not only your
own loving and unworthy Susan, but a
Countess, with the dignity of generations
of noble ladies to maintain."

"If you only knew how at this moment
I fear to lose you, how the past starts up
before me, with its lonely watches by the
soldier's camp fire, its weary marches in

foreign lands, its longing to hear again the sound of your dear voice!"

"My dear Oliver!" she says, as he looks into her eloquent eyes, that speak in fervent gaze her deep-seated love.

"I sometimes dream," he went on, "that seas again roll on between us; how another has snatched you from me; and in a passion of mad sorrow I find you at last only in time to hear the bells ring out a wild endorsement of its truth—they have given you to another!"

She takes his hand and kisses it, her hot tears falling the while.

"And so they did, Oliver; but not my heart! That could not happen even in a dream. You do right to rebuke me."

"Nay, my dearest, I would not have you think I would rebuke you."

"Can I ever forget your noble, manly

words, your look of suffering pride in that day when I had sunk so low!"

He raises her head between his two hands and kisses her.

"Susan," he says, "I would not have you weep for all the world! Let us wait for years rather than you should think there is a rebuke in my impatience. We are young, the world is bright and gay about us; do but say you forgive me that I brought tears into your eyes, and bid me wait until doomsday."

"My own dear, generous Oliver!" she says. "That was Father Busby whose shadow fell upon the terrace this moment; he is coming this way; he is bound up in my interest and happiness; he shall decide for us; let us go and meet him."

As they leave the room by way of the terrace, there enters by the door a servant, followed by Lawyer Dobbs.

"You should have waited, sir, in the library," says the servant.

"My business is too urgent for that."

"Well, Mr. Hardwick is walking in the grounds. Since you are following me about like my shadow, sir, you had better come this way; I daresay he is feeding the animals."

"I would like to feed them with his carcase," mumbled Dobbs.

"Beg your pardon, sir ?"

"Oh, nothing; lead me to him."

They have hardly disappeared by the right, down the terrace steps, when Oliver and Susan return by the left, and with them Father Busby. He is speaking upon the momentous question of their marriage, as they walk into the room, Susan on one side of him, Oliver on the other.

"My dear children," he is saying, "the

circumstances that surround you are so entirely exceptional that I think the position may be treated exceptionally, and I see no reason for delay."

"Father Busby," says Oliver, "I am almost inclined to embrace you and your Faith too, for that answer; I do approve of your principles in this question most heartily."

"And you have no strong objection to those of our religion, have you, Oliver?" asks Susan, her eyes bent upon the ground.

"Nay, I could be a Mahomedan for your sake, Susan."

"Forgive him, Father! Soldiers were ever profane, except on the eve of battle," says Susan.

"And they worship trinkets, ribbons, and locks of hair," answers Oliver.

"Captain North is merry, and little blame to him, Countess," says the Father, "but whom have we here; and in angry altercation ?"

"My father and Lawyer Dobbs," exclaims Susan, as the two enter the room, Dobbs taking off his hat and bending low as he enters.

"My dear," says Mr. Hardwick, "here is Mr. Dobbs, who has no longer any business with yourself or with me, who has been directed to hand over his papers to Mr. Mercer, who has no right whatever to address us in person, who was ordered to direct any communication that he might have to make upon our affairs to our new solicitor; he comes here declaring that he will do nothing of the kind, and insisting upon our withdrawing these orders, declaring he will stay here until we do, and uttering all kinds of threats. I must invoke your personal authority in the business——"

Hardwick is quite out of breath with passion and indignation at the affront which he and the Countess sustained in the unbidden presence of his arch-enemy and former ally, Septimus Dobbs.

"Pardon me a moment," says Susan to Oliver and Father Busby, who stand aside and converse together.

" I did not desire to trespass upon you, Countess, especially at so interesting a moment," says Dobbs, glancing in the direction of North and Father Busby.

" Then pray withdraw your presence from us," says the Countess, " and address yourself to the solicitor and agent my father has appointed. It is not my wish that this change should be a serious money loss to you, and I shall ask you to name a sum which you think will be a fair compensation for the loss of this business."

"It is not a question of money, it is a question of position, reputation, dignity," answers Dobbs; "which cannot be estimated in money."

"No, truly," says the Countess.

"This is a fight that must be fought with kindred weapons. Your father has brought about my discomfiture from motives of malice and revenge. He shall be answered like by like. I could tell you a story that would tame you both!"

"Sir, leave this place!" exclaims Hardwick, and, as he speaks, sounds of many voices are heard in the grounds.

"Do you order me to go?"

"Yes."

"And who are you?"

"The master of this house," says Hardwick.

Dobbs lays his hat ostentatiously upon the floor and takes a seat, at which Oliver North steps forward, but pauses to hear the Countess say,

"At least, sir, I am mistress here, and I order you to go !"

"What is the meaning of it ?" suddenly exclaims Father Busby ; " there is a crowd of men rushing over the lawn and coming this way."

"They are coming to see me turned out," says Dobbs, with a mocking laugh, and an insulting gesture towards the Countess.

"Then, by heavens ! they shall not be disappointed," exclaims Oliver North, seizing him by the collar of his coat, literally carrying him across the room, and pitching him into the arms of some score of men who are hurrying up the terrace, headed by a leader, who, pausing at the entrance of the open windows to wave a halt with his hand, steps inside the room, Dobbs crawling in after him.

"Forgive this sudden and uninvited intrusion!" says the foremost man, raising his hat with the grace of a gentleman and bowing to the Countess.

It was a startling surprise for all of them, this appearance of Scruton; for, despite the change in him, they all recognized him on the instant. He was dressed almost, as it appeared, in the same clothes as those he wore when last they had seen him; and he had fortified himself with wine almost to madness, which helped the identity.

"I see you know me!" he says, advancing, "Philip Scruton, Earl of Ellerbie, proprietor of this house. Pray don't be disturbed; you are heartily welcome here, though I did not invite you."

Then, turning specially to the priest, he bows his head.

"Father, your blessing!"

The priest turns away.

"You will give it me anon," says Scruton; "but be seated, Countess, and you, Mr. North—Captain North, I believe—and you, Mr. Hardwick, be seated; don't let me break up your domestic harmony."

There is a bitter irony in his tone and manner. Susan fears him. She nestles close to the side of Oliver North, and well she may; for Scruton looks like the devil himself. His eyes are bloodshot, his face sallow, his thin lips and cruel mouth look the wickeder for his coal-black moustache and thin straggling imperial.

At the beckoning of his finger a constable comes forward from the crowd on the terrace and goes up to North.

"I am sorry to arrest you, Mr. North,

but it is my duty; here is my warrant."

"Arrest me!" exclaims North.

"Arrest you!" gasps Susan, clinging to his arm, and looking appealingly at Father Busby.

By this time the butler and most of the Countess's servants have entered the room.

"Hear my orders," says Scruton, addressing them; "hear the orders of your master, Lord Ellerbie!"

They stare at him and at everybody in dumb amazement.

"The rooms of the Countess and her venerable father remain at their entire disposal; the carriages, horses, all that I possess at Brackenbury will remain at present to the use and under the command of the Countess. Go, give meat and drink to those tenants and friends you see yonder, who are here to join you in welcoming your lost lord home again!"

Not one of them moves, at which the crowd grows impatient and presses into the room, two other constables coming forward as Scruton beckons them.

" What is the meaning of this ?" says Susan, at last, summoning all her courage, Oliver North being now surrounded, and appearing for the moment paralysed with astonishment. " Of what is that innocent, honest, brave gentleman and my future husband charged ?"

" Of the murder of the late Lord Ellerbie !" answers Scruton, raising his voice, a malicious smile on his lips as Susan staggers fainting into the arms of her lover.

" Ruffian !" exclaims North, thrusting aside the constables and holding up his fainting charge, who is at once attended by her women, " you shall live to repent this day and die miserably as you have lived !"

"Officers, see to your prisoner!" says Scruton, turning his back upon him to consult with Dobbs, who shuffles up to his new master, and then going to the crowd leads off "three cheers for the returned exile, and welcome home again to the Earl of Ellerbie!"

CHAPTER VI.

SERGEANT-MAJOR TOM BERTRAM IS VERY BUSY.

GOWAN.—Beg thy pardon, thou popinjay! Dost
think, an thou wearest silken hose and danglest a
sword of Spain on thy skimpy thigh, I'll beg thy
pardon?

SIR RICHARD.—Marry, knave, an thou dost not fall
straightway on thy knees, I'll run that same rapier
through thy misbegotten carcase.

THERE could be no question about the
rights of the returned heir. Scruton
was undoubtedly Lord Ellerbie.

"And the very last this time!" said Mrs.
Kirk.

"That remains to be seen," said the farmer.

"Well, if he doesn't get killed or drownded, or something, there's no justice this side the grave," said the dame.

"We've seen it overtake a villain when least expected," said Kirk; "bide your time, missus."

"Ah, but the devil takes care on his own," she answered.

"For a time, maybe," answered the farmer; "but he gets tired of waiting for 'em, and drags 'em down at last."

"Well, well, it would seem as if the honest and true have a hard time of it. To think of another innocent, brave, good young fellow being in danger of his neck on a false charge!"

"I wonnat believe he's in danger!"

"You said so when poor Jacob Marks was took up."

"I did, I did. But it wouldna be safe to hurt a hair of Captain North's head. There'd be a riot; blame me, if I donnat think there would be a revolution."

"Oh, I donnat know," said Mrs. Kirk. "Folk have a way of knocking under to things when law and constables and soldiers is again' a man."

Tom Bertram and Mary came into the Home Farm while the two old people were talking. The young couple were on their way to Brackenbury. They had only just heard the startling news of Scruton's return and Oliver North's arrest. North had been taken in a carriage to the House of Correction or gaol at Chesterfield. Tom was overwhelmed with anxiety, and would not even "cheer up" under Mary Kirk's liveliest sallies concerning the advantages a man possessed who, having only one eye, could concentrate his entire vision upon any given subject. Mary argued that it was no good for everybody to be "down in the dumps"—they must go and see what was to be done. Thank goodness, she did not despair, and she was used to troubles and difficulties and surprises !

Mary found Susan utterly broken down, but nevertheless directing, though like one in a dream, the business of her removal and her father's to the Hall. Old Hardwick had actually counselled her remaining at the Towers, for a time, at least, and she had not spoken to him since. He had said to the butler that it was kind of his lordship to give orders for the Countess's commands to be obeyed. He had even sought a private interview with the new lord " to talk matters over," and had listened with patience to Scruton when he said the best thing his daughter could do would be to accept him as her husband.

He had gone further—he had intimated that time might favour the new lord's suit.

"By the saints, old man!" Scruton had said, pushing the bottle over to Hardwick (Dobbs had gone to Chesterfield with the prisoner), "if you could bring that about, there is nothing she could ask of me that she should not have!"

Hardwick had not gone so far as even to glance a hint at such a mad proposal to Susan; but he had said he thought it would be wise that they should not leave Brackenbury at least for a few days.

"For which remark I shall never forgive you!" said Susan; whereupon the old time-serving scoundrel had whimpered and pretended to cry, muttering all the time that he only lived for her welfare, for her happiness.

Neither his snivelling nor his professions of love moved her.

"I will never forgive you!" she repeated.

"And she never ought!" said Mary Kirk, who was present, and who burned to give Mr. Hardwick a piece of her mind.

Messengers had been sent to get the Hall in order, and by sunset a waggon from Tom Bertram's farm and two hackney coaches from Chesterfield were drawn up before the western entrance of Brackenbury Towers, the waggon packed with trunks, the coaches for the Countess, her maid, and Mary, and another vehicle for Mr. Hardwick; for Susan had declined to use either horses or carriages belonging to Brackenbury Towers, and she left the place with no more than she had brought there. Hardwick was in sore distress at this. Even Mary Kirk did not approve of Susan leaving behind the family jewels, the famous Ellerbie diamonds; but Susan was resolute, she would not touch a stone of them.

"They are her own," whimpered Hardwick to Mrs. Tom Bertram; "she is still the Countess, and Brackenbury is settled upon her; she is demented; my daughter is mad!"

When Susan and Mary had left the Countess's apartments, and gone down stairs to take their places in the hackney coach, old Hardwick had run through the rooms and scrambled together all the jewellery he could lay his hands on, thrusting it into one of his own trunks, where he had also concealed several bottles of the green seal madeira, and many articles of no value whatever, just as people at a fire will save hair-brushes, hand-glasses, trifling ornaments, anything that comes first to hand, while leaving behind them valuable treasures.

As Mary and Susan were passing through the great hall, they were confronted by Scruton.

"One word," he said, "in *his* interest, not in mine."

Susan would have hurried past him, but Mary held her back.

"Hear what he has to say," said Mary; "he may be going to confess his villainy and release his victim."

"Thank you, my pert mistress," said Scruton, "not so fast nor so malicious. But if this is to be farewell to Brackenbury, the host should be allowed a parting word."

"Let me go, Mary," said Susan; "his presence is an insult."

"I can save Captain North," said the villain; "it rests with you."

"There! Listen, my dear friend," said Mary, "for his sake, for Oliver's sake."

"Go on, sir," said Susan.

"I would speak with you alone!" answered Scruton.

"You waste your time, then, and ours," said Susan.

"I won't listen; speak," said Mary.

Scruton looked round, and closed an adjacent door.

"It is a bold thing I have to say, and you may resent it now; but you will, perhaps, think it over afterwards and discuss it with your friend, who seems to have judgment."

"If it concerns Captain North's interest," said Mary, "the Countess will attend; go on, Mr. Scruton."

"Not Mr. Scruton now, pretty one, Lord Ellerbie, mistress," said the vagabond.

"Don't 'pretty one' me," said Mary; "my husband may cudgel you else, if you were fifty times Lord Ellerbie."

"Say you so?" he replied, trying to smile pleasantly, but only distorting his already Satanic features.

Susan had sunk upon a chair by Mary's side, her face in her hands; and Tom Bertram might have been seen twice to look in upon them imapatiently, for the wagon was loaded, and the horses were pawing the earth.

"Believe me, I feel for the Countess," he said, "falling from such a height; but it is not my wish that her position should be lowered. On the contrary, an Ellerbie was her choice. He gave her wealth, a title, all that women desire, except a husband near her own age, a gallant of whom she could feel proud. Let the past be forgotten. Let me be the Ellerbie of her choice!"

Gradually raising her head as he spoke, Susan sprang to her feet.

"Oh!" she exclaimed, "I am fallen indeed ! Is there no one to protect me from this shame, this insult?"

"Why, surely!" said Tom Bertram, who had been gradually convinced, as he stood in the shadow of the porch, that things were becoming unpleasant both for his wife and the Countess, "there's me! What is it?"

"Tom!" cried Susan, rushing to him.

"Don't be afraid!" said Tom.

"Take me away!"

"That I will," said Bertram.

Scruton rushed between Susan and Tom, cutting off the women from their protector.

"Now, sir, beg my pardon!" shouted the Earl.

"For what?" asked Tom, shifting his position so that he got the enemy on his light side.

"For this intrusion."

"Let me put the ladies into the coach

and so I will, if it please you to think I've done anything wrong," said Tom. "That's fair, your lordship."

Tom was so humble that Scruton, thrown off his guard, allowed him, as the ladies were now by Tom's side again, to conduct them out of the hall.

"You won't go back, Tom, dear Tom!" said Mary, as Tom handed them into the carriage and pulled down the steps.

"Don't you be afraid, little one," he said, closing the window, and telling the coachman to drive on.

Then, picking up an ash stick lying by his wagon, he directed his man to drive on too, saying he would overtake him.

"Now, sir!" he said, rushing back through the porch and into the hall, where Scruton was still standing alone, fuming and fretting, in a rage with himself, and half maddened with drink, "what am I to beg your pardon for?"

"Because I choose to wish it, peasant!" said Scruton, with studied insolence.

"Shall you call your lackeys if I don't?"

"No."

"Shall you if I do? For they'd come if you did; they don't mind who they serve, it seems!"

"What do you mean, you impertinent cur?" said Scruton, his hand upon his sword.

"That if you will undertake we be not disturbed, I will tell you something I heard in Paris; but I don't want to be detained here—I've gotten to see after my wagon."

"You are a cool knave," answered Scruton. "My servants will not come unless I call them."

"They said in my regiment, quartered

in Paris, that you are a cheat, a liar, and a coward!"

Scruton whipped out his sword, and his hand trembled as the sturdy yeoman faced him.

"I don't know if you are a cheat, I never played with you; I know you are a coward, for I heard you insult a lady: and I know you are a liar, for you said I should beg your pardon!"

"Damn you!" exclaimed Scruton, making an ugly and cowardly pass at Tom, which the young fellow had been fully prepared for all the time, and which he parried vigorously with his stick, that came down the next moment with such force upon Scruton's pate that the new Earl dropped prone upon his family oak.

"Well done, Tom!" said the sergeant to himself, as he contemplated the prostrate foe; "as pretty a bit of sword practice as man could desire, thanks to the activity of one eye and the strength of Mary's bracelet."

Tom picked up the sword.

"You misbegotten sinner!" he said, apostrophising the vanquished foe, "if you were in Spain or some other civilised country, I think I could have the heart to stick it through your gizzard!"

Instead of doing so, he laid out the lappet of Scruton's coat and pinned it to the oaken floor. Then he took from his pocket a piece of chalk and wrote, in a big round hand :—

"*Here lyes A coward who drawed on a Unarmed Man and if he is Lord Ellerbie I am his Tenant And this is how I gives him Notice to quit. Tom Bertram, late Sergeant-Major in His Majesty's Royals.*"

Scruton sighed and began to move as Tom finished.

" There, I've done it !" said the yeoman,
"been and ruined myself, I suppose, and
Mary too ; well, dang me, I cannot help it !
A man as has fought for his country and
is down for medals and things is not going
to be put upon by a damned gasconading
villain like that, earl or no earl !"

Tom marched down the long avenue and
into the high-road with an elastic tread.
He almost fancied he could hear the
band of his old regiment playing " Rule
Britannia."

"The foreign-looking whelp !" he said,
" the spider-legged ill-favoured devil, to
come his outlandish airs on me ! And to
try to set his ugly self up in Captain
North's place, and that poor fellow by this
time in that there hole of a prison on the
Hipper ! I'll tell you what, my fine
Frenchy earl, with your dancing-pumps
and your fancy sword, if anything happens

to Oliver North, look out! I've had the
settling of one villain, against my will,
that was; but I'll button you up, Mester
Scruton, as sure as I am Grassmoor born
and bred!"

He strode on, talking to himself and
flourishing his stick. Presently he stopped, as if to hold a council of war.

"But look here, Tom, you monnat go
on talking like that!" he said. "You are
forgetting that blessed little wife of yourn;
you mon't go and get yoursen into trouble,
else what'll she do? That's the worst of
being married, it cripples you when feight-
ing and such-like comes in; but there, I
munnat forget Mary, bless her; I wouldn't
give her a minute's trouble for—there, I
donnat know what! But, dang it, I'm
glad I whipped that bragging, foreign-
lookin' catamaran!"

Tom called on his way at the Home

Farm, and told Kirk what he had done.

"Don't tell the missus, lad!" said Kirk. "I'm sorry thou did it; that is, I'm sorry it had to be done!"

"Ah, that's it!" said Tom, "it had to be done, father-in-law."

"And as it had to be done, son-in-law, I'm glad thou didst it well!"

"What do you think he'll do about it?"

"It's hard to say. Nowt, if he isn't a born fool."

"Well, it isna a thing to brag about, eh?" said Tom, laughing aloud; "maybe he'll keep it to himsen."

"But you'll have to leave farm," said Kirk; "it's a reight down good thing I've getten my own freehold. There's missus coming."

"I wonnat stay," said Tom, hurrying off; "I shall be sure to let it out if I stop."

He strode out for Chesterfield, turning out of his way to take a look at the Miller and his Men, for he was in a strange kind of humour. The old place was half pulled down, and the labourers were just leaving work for the day.

"Owner's going to build a new mill on spot," said the foreman, "and Bow Street runner chap's been here, and we've found among other things marked guineas hidden under floor of Short's bed-room—them guineas as poor Marks was hanged for stealing."

"You donnat say so!" exclaimed Tom. "Well, well! And yet that same fellow, a Hearl he is now, as was robbed and swore again Marks is now on another innocent man to get him hanged."

"Ay, we've heard about Captain North," said the foreman.

"Well, you'd niver stand harm being

done to him, eh, wonld any on us, after this business of them guineas, and this Mister Lawyer Dobbs at work in it again?"

"No, I think there would be a row," said the foreman, and the men standing round said, "Ay, there would."

"Did you ever see a thieving son of a gun drummed out of a regiment?" Tom asked.

"No."

"Well, it's a sight! You just tak' him —he's done summat, mind you, as bad as a chap like Dobbs would—and you first strip off his stripes and buttons and things, and you just kick him out while band plays 'Rogue's March.' I'd like to treat Mr. Dobbs to the ugly march, and kick him out of Chesterfield and the county that way."

"Ay," the men said, "so would we."

"Well, shall we do it, lads, one day?"
Tom asked.

"Ay," they said.

"And will you let me be captain of
Kicking-out Army?"

"Ay, lad!" they shouted, laughing merrily; "but donnat delay it long."

"No, I wonnat," said Tom. "Good
night, lads!" And on he marched, apostrophising himself again. "Tom, lad," he
said, "thou mun mind thy eye. Thou
wilt surely get into trouble if thou doesna
mind."

When he arrived at Chesterfield, he
found the town in a commotion. There
were crowds in the streets. Quite a mul-
titude were round the old Hall. He made
a surveillance, and, finding all well there,
he went on to the Angel. The greatest
indignation was expressed there at the
arrest of North. Susan Jane was in high

feather, for her evidence, it was held, was enough to exculpate him on the spot. Dick Holmes had not left the Angel all day. His business, people were saying, would go to the dogs. And so it might, he said. He wanted to be married, and Susan Jane had been forced, under threats of bankruptcy, suicide, and every horror under the sun, to vow that she would marry Dick the day Oliver North married the Countess of Ellerbie—a vow which stimulated Dick's faith in Oliver's innocence, and his hope of a speedy manifestation thereof.

Tom found that, though there were two sides touching the question of the rights and wrongs of Oliver's arrest, the side that was against him was a poor little shabby minority of tradesmen, who were content to be bought, body and soul, by the reigning power at Brackenbury. There was a strong feeling growing up against Scruton and Dobbs, and, when the report of Scruton's appearance in the fair began to be discussed in detail, many cried shame on those who had consented to drink the liquor of the man who had insulted them. The story of Billy Nipper and his sister was told; and one man said Nannie Lomas was ready to take her oath that Dobbs knew the fellow was coming; that Dobbs and Scruton had arranged it all, so that the vagabond might seem to have been badly treated by the late Earl, and make a sensation of it, so as to get sympathy, and folks to go up to Brackenbury with him.

"Ah! you wait," Nannie had said; "you'll see summat yet as will oppen your eyes along of Mester Dobbs and his new mester! It wasn't wise getting North locked up; but folks never is wise when they lets their feelings get better of their judgment."

Those were the words which it was reported Nannie had used.

"And she knows!" said Dick Holmes. "If ever there was a witch she's one, and it's a good thing for her as she didna live when my owd grandfayther were alive; they'd have had her in the river Hipper swimmin' for it!"

Tom went down to the House of Correction, miserably situated on that same river, in the lower part of the town. The gaoler would not let Tom see North, because he said a gentleman from London was with him, and under no circumstances were they to be disturbed.

"A gentleman from London," said Tom; "but I'm his old friend."

"Ay, it doesna matter," said the gaoler.

"But I come from the Countess of Ellerbie."

"Nay, that's a whacker!"

"What do you mean?"

"Why, she's only just gone."

"Has she been here?"

"I should think she has."

"How long since?"

"Why, she's only just gone, crowd after her cheering like mad."

"Ay, I thought there weren't many folk about here."

"No, not now; they've followed lady-ship's carriage I tell thee, shouting them-selves hoarse, saying, 'Never mind,' 'Cheer up,' 'He'll get off,' 'We'n have that there Dobbs in his place,' and such like things, and constable's been here afraid as there will be a riot; we'n have to get sowjers from Sheffield if there is."

"Ah! I reckon so. And who's chap

from London as is with Captain North?"

"Well, I donnat know as there's any secret about it; he's pretty well known by this time in Chesterfield, a-coming and going in a sort of herratic way, Mr. Spelter, the famous Bow Street Runner."

"Oh!" said Tom, his face lighting up with a pleased expression—"oh! Mester Spelter, that's all right, I can sleep in comfort then; Spelter, oh! ah! well! Then I'll come and see Captain in the morning, eh?"

"Yes," said the gaoler; "he'll go before magistrate to-morrow."

"Mester Dick Spelter, eh? Oh! well, that's good news, I'm sure. So good night, Mester, good night!"

His stick under his arm, his hands in his pockets, Tom now took a short cut for Lordsmill Street and the Hall, where Mary was anxiously awaiting him.

"Nannie Lomas is again' both Dobbs and new lordship," he said, talking to himself as he strode along; "and if Spelter's having a confab with Oliver, Spelter's on Oliver's side. I'm glad I had a run round; I've picked up nowt but good news. Eh, but I should like to tell her about my fine gentleman skewered to floor and ticketed with my notice to quit. But I suppose I monnat just yet; I mun be sly about it for present, till I see what comes on it."

CHAPTER VII.

SPELTER AT WORK.

Foul deeds will rise,
Though all the earth o'erwhelm them, to men's eyes.
SHAKSPERE.

PHILIP SCRUTON, Earl of Ellerbie,
concluded to say nothing about the
reverse he had sustained in his encounter
with Tom Bertram, Sergeant-Major; but
to take his revenge when opportunity
offered.

Moreover, Philip Scruton, Earl of Ellerbie, was too much engaged from the moment he came to his senses until night (one might truly say until the close of his career) to afford any time to think about his daring assailant. For the first person Philip Scruton, Earl of Ellerbie, saw when he scrambled to his feet was that clerical brother of the strange Order who had first crossed his tortuous path in London, shortly after the meeting with Dobbs at the Cock Tavern in Fleet Street; and whom he had once encountered since that time in Madrid, whither the chiefs had summoned him to answer for certain shortcomings, not to say disregard of vows and contempt of warnings.

The secret societies of Europe counted among their powerful associations no more formidable combination, political and religious, than that into which Philip Scruton had been sworn; and none adhered more closely to the fulfilment of its sanguinary ritual of punishment in the event of dis-

loyalty. Philip Scruton had had reason to
know how far-reaching was its power;
and conciliation as well as policy had
entered into his plans when he left England
for the Continent the day following the
murder of his uncle—left secretly and dis-
guised, to return openly, as we have already witnessed. Though he believed he
had made his peace, the Council of Three
had despatched the mysterious brother
aforesaid in his wake, with instructions
that were not uttered, but conveyed in a
penal sign, coupled with that of caution.
This officer of the order had himself, beyond his duty and his office, a personal
enmity towards Scruton. " We shall meet
again," he had said to the derelict brother
at the close of Scruton's interrogations on
that long past day near Hyde Park. " We
meet again !" was the priest's salutation in
Madrid when Scruton knelt before the

Council of Three, confessed his breaches, and promised amendment. "For the third time, Brother of the Third Grade," he said, as he contemplated the new Earl tearing his coat from the ignominious stab of his own sword, "we meet again!"

Scruton passed his hand over his face and stared at his visitor, the last person in the world whom he had expected to see. The foreigner was attired now in semi-clerical garb, and looked the part he was playing—that of a Romish priest.

"*Here lyes A coward who drawed on a Unarmed Man and if he is Lord Ellerbie I am his Tenant And this is how I gives him Notice to quit. Tom Bertram, late Sergeant-Major in His Majesty's Royals*," said the priest, tracing the writing on the floor with his long black cane.

"The cursed knave! it was he who took *me* at a disadvantage," said Scruton, rubbing his feet upon the offensive chalk marks.

"Indeed!" said the brother from Madrid.

"But why are you here?" he asked.

"To see Father Busby," answered the priest.

"I thought we were outside his pale," said Scruton.

"The orthodox Church only recognizes us on special occasions. I come on an exceptional mission. Will you conduct me?"

"May I know the nature of your mission?"

"You may not."

Scruton bowed and led the way. In the library he called a servant.

"A visitor for Father Busby," said Scruton.

"This way, your reverence," answered the servant; and in due course the Spaniard was closeted with the faithful chaplain of the Ellerbies.

"I neither recognize your order, nor its mission, since both are under the ban of Holy Church; but, setting aside your Order, and leaving the sin of disobedience to His Holiness, I may respond to your other claim; and since, individually, the members of your Brotherhood are not excommunicate, I give you welcome!" said Father Busby, after some preliminary overtures of friendship and priestly brotherhood.

"It is of the Earl who has just seized, as it were, title and estates I would ask you."

"He has done ill in the violence of his possession; but he is the rightful heir," said Father Busby.

"Though His Holiness doth put us outside the light of his benign countenance,

we feel no less our duty to our Mother
Church ; would it not have been better for
thee and her that the holy crusade should
have been fought with the aid of our new
sister in the Faith than with this heir who
cometh and goeth so violently ?"

"I gather no hope of righteous advance-
ment for the Church under the auspices of
Lord Ellerbie. The widow of his uncle is
a meet instrument for good, and I had
hoped God Himself had given her to the
Cause ;·for a more devoted recruit never
joined our sacred banner."

The Spaniard disappeared from Brackenbury almost as mysteriously as he came ;
but Dick Spelter was not surprised to see
him soon afterwards at his modest retreat
by the Horns tavern.

"The highwayman who disclosed to you

the character of Short confessed at my instigation," said the foreigner.

"And many thanks for the same—remember you coming into prison to confess him," said Spelter.

"Your mission to the Miller and his Men brought you in timely connection with Brackenbury?"

"It did—unlucky with Short—too late with Short—a little fogged with Brackenbury," said Spelter.

" No, you are not."

"Oh, well, come, if you know better than me, out with it—you gents do get hold of things somehow—if we in the thief-taking profession only had your confessional privileges!"

" You would never convict a prisoner," said the Spaniard, quickly. "There are black sheep in all professions, Mr. Spelter, but not in all the history of the Church has priest ever yielded up the secret of the confessional."

"Dick Spelter is an ignorant fool—he begs your pardon—there!"

"Why do you halt in this business of Brackenbury?"

"Why do I halt? Well, that's a leading question—what do you mean?"

The priest made no reply.

"A man can't run an affair like this down all in a minute—must communicate with superiors sometimes—extraordinary business this—create sensation all through country—Spelter must make no mistake."

"Spelter shall not," said the priest.

"Thanks again—very good of you to watch over Spelter."

"If the officer, whose fame has even reached Spain and Germany, trifles with his reputation, it is fitting that the friend, who pointed him the way to a higher distinction than that he has yet won, should come to his aid."

"Oh! you are an oddity—but I like oddities—I like you—a man who pulls me up the moment I see him—sets me thinking—makes me feel I'm in superior company—that man has my respect—pardon me, but you must be in the profession, eh? —now come, reverend sir—eh?"

"I am on my way to London, thence to the Continent. I heard you were here—"

"Yes, and very good of you to look me up—feel honoured—should like to return the compliment when I cross the Channel."

"And I find you," went on the priest, not noticing Spelter's remark, "hesitating when you should strike, pausing on the threshold of success when you should go boldly in. Shall I call on the Duke of York and explain to his Grace the new outrage which has been committed in Derbyshire by the arrest of an innocent man on a charge as false as that which hanged one Jacob Marks, casting shame and scandal on the administration of justice in this part of the kingdom?"

"You know His Royal Highness?"

"I know all your masters, royal and ministerial," said the priest.

"One of us," touching himself on the breast, "only of a higher grade—felt sure of it when you come into Horsemonger Lane—says I, 'Spelter, he's a—' well, never mind, it ain't a word you might like, though not intended disrespectful—don't be impatient—the arrest of Oliver North ain't my affair—nothing to do with it—told Lawyer Dobbs it was wrong."

"Then tell Lawyer Dobbs what is right," said the priest, "and good day, Mr. Spelter!"

" I have the honour to wish you a pleasant journey," said Spelter, opening the
door.

" Comes and goes just like them high-
handed ones—spy, should think he was—
no more a priest, I dessay, than I am—a
Government spy—clever chaps, them foreign gentlemen—such an advantage speaking another language too—the gift of
tongues—well, Spelter, you take the tip
when it's given you straight—tell Lawyer
Dobbs what is right, so I will—bounce
him, Spelter, my boy—bounce him; you've
had a good deal of his coin—bounce him!"

" Sure can't be overheard ?" said Spelter,
sitting by the fire in Dobbs's office.

" Certain."

" Close all the doors."

Dobbs closed them.

" Lock 'em !"

Dobbs locked them.

"Not a soul within a room and a passage of us?"

"Not a soul," said Dobbs.

"Things look ugly. You should not have permitted that arrest."

"No, I felt it was wrong."

"Will bring things to a crisis."

"Yes?"

"You've paid me a good deal of money during the business."

"You have earned it, Spelter."

"Perhaps; but my reputation's at stake now—must consider reputation—man in the play, you know, awful way about his reputation. You are nervous, Mr. Dobbs—don't look well."

"I am not well," said Dobbs.

"Do you remember me telling you it was a murder, at first? Do you remember I said I'd find the two men?"

" Two men !" repeated Dobbs. " Did you say two ?"

" Always said two—don't you call to mind I said we must first find the motive —first consider who benefited most ?"

" North would benefit if he married the widow," said Dobbs.

" You really look very ill," said Spelter ; " take a little of something—brandy's a good thing."

" No, no, not now—business first," said Dobbs.

" Sure we can't be overheard—mysteri-ous business going on—Government spy at my place an hour ago—strange messages to me from London—don't want you to criminate yourself, as you would say, sir —but——"

" What do you mean ?" asked Dobbs, rising, and trying to assume an indignant tone and manner.

"To be as pleasant as I've always been—but plainer-spoken—more to the purpose—don't be foolish, Dobbs—you've paid me well, and I'm not ungrateful."

Dobbs could not fail to notice the unaccustomed tone of familiarity which Spelter assumed towards him. Coupled with the detective's persistent caution about probable listeners, it filled Dobbs with terror; for he had only just packed up the Scruton deeds and securities in his strong box, and he had not forgotten how plainly Scruton had given him to understand that they were confederates.

"Well, Mr. Spelter," said Dobbs, "we have been good friends, and I have tried to do my best in fulfilling the duties and responsibilities that have lain in my way; and with Heaven's blessing I hope to continue to do so."

"Don't preach," said Spelter, quickly—

"it makes me uncomfortable—not, like the devil in the play, on account of fear—just the opposite—what I want you to consider is this—and me being, as it were, partly in your service, since you have generously paid many of my expenses, you being steward, lawyer, and family adviser of the Ellerbies in one—I feel it is right to let you know where we stand."

" Yes, truly, and I am the more beholden to you, Mr. Spelter," said Dobbs.

" Try a little brandy now," said Spelter, "and I will join you—know you do keep it handy—or wouldn't ask you—also know it's old as Methuselah or shouldn't touch it—no smuggled liquor for me—as I was saying——"

Dobbs, turning to a small cupboard behind his chair, produced a bottle and wine glasses, and they both sipped the liquor unwatered.

"It is fine, no doubt about it," said Spelter. "Well, you see, Mr. Dobbs, as I was saying, I have now my reputation to consider—my reputation demands that I clear up this Brackenbury business straight —can do it without your aid—with your aid can do it in such a way as will be more satisfactory to you."

"I am sure I can rely on your friendship," said Dobbs.

"Now the business stands thus—am making sacrifice to friendship in showing you my hand—hope you'll appreciate it— now observe."

Spelter raised his left hand, spreading out fingers and thumb. "No. 1—Your clandestine meetings with Scruton in London and the sham announcements of his death." (Spelter pressed his thumb.) "No. 2—The robbery of Oliver North not only of a ribbon, but a knife—keep your mind on the knife." (Spelter pressed down his first finger, and Dobbs sat speechless.) " No. 3—Scruton's purchase of a masquerading costume and his leaving London a week before the murder of Lord Ellerbie." (The second finger down.) " No. 4—The secret passage and the murder !" (Dobbs watched Spelter put down the third finger with a certain fascination of fear.) " No. 5—That sneaking clerk of yours who engrossed the deeds of consideration from Scruton to yourself."

" What !" exclaimed Dobbs, his lip quivering.

" Don't get excited—attend, and judge the situation as if you were counsel engaged for Septimus Dobbs—as if Lawyer Dobbs was your client—as if Mr. Dobbs had criminated himself in some way—say he is in trouble, and you were engaged to get him out."

"I am attending," Dobbs replied, his mouth becoming suddenly dry, his tongue parched, and his hands deadly cold.

"The prosecution, say, runs over its case, enumerates its witnesses—waiter from the Cock Tavern—sly person that waiter—supposed old soldier who robbed North—Mr. Hardwick, who has confessed to his desire for that ribbon, and your undertaking to get it for him—old soldier should not have taken knife as well—mistake for Dobbs to let Scruton get hold of knife—Nannie Lomas, who is a witch, that's certain—newspaper man who produces your written account of Scruton's death—footmarks in the secret passage and by the lake that fit Scruton's boots —your ungrateful clerk, who has from time to time given me access to your papers——"

Dobbs started, all trembling, to his feet.

"Sit down—be calm—you are not Dobbs just now, remember, but his counsel—and lastly a witness who has some mysterious power over the case in general, and information more curious than that of Nannie Lomas herself—he is a Spanish priest —and the daring conclusion of the whole —now listen, Dobbs's counsel—take note, most learned counsel of the accused—the charge is that Scruton murdered his uncle, and that Septimus Dobbs was accessory before and after the fact!"

As he concluded, Spelter fixed his keen little eyes upon Dobbs and rose solemnly from his chair, the lawyer falling back and staring blankly at the detective.

"Strong case, eh, counsel for Dobbs? —what is Dobbs to do?—Scruton being in custody——"

"In custody!" gasped Dobbs, both hands clinging to the arms of the chair in which he was sitting.

"I said in custody—the principal in this horrible murder being in custody——"

"It was North we arrested," said Dobbs, turning livid with anxiety.

"North *you* arrested—yes, that was another of the mistakes of Dobbs—make a note of it, Dobbs's counsel."

"I did not," gasped Dobbs.

"Dobbs did not arrest North, it is true," said Spelter, persisting in addressing the shrinking wretch as if he were his own counsel; "but he allowed the malice of Scruton to go so far—just as he permitted North's knife to fall into Scruton's hands —Scruton reckless person—guard of a local coach remembers night of murder dropping man dressed like a Jew pedlar near Hasland—same height as Scruton—

two servants at Brackenbury now remember him coming to the Hall—the costumier who clothed him is already in Chesterfield —no doubt whatever who killed Lord Ellerbie—and the coward who did it is coward enough to implicate his pal—consider that, my learned friend."

"Whom should you charge with being his pal, as you call him?" asked Dobbs, slowly, his eyes wandering in a vain effort to fix them calmly on Spelter's face.

" Septimus Dobbs," said Spelter.

Dobbs's head sank upon his breast. His fingers worked nervously.

" What should I do if I were in Dobbs's place?" said the detective, as if he had been asked the question. "I should say, Dick Spelter, you are a friend to me, and I thank you—as long as your reputation was not at stake you kept things quiet— and when your reputation and honour come

into play you give me the office—what I
should do if I was Mister Dobbs is this,
knowing what a scoundrel I have to deal
with in Scruton, whose character is of the
very worst as is—I should not wait till
poor kind-hearted Spelter is obliged to
arrest me on the capital charge, and, when
arrested, might not be allowed to turn
King's evidence, because Spelter has
enough evidence to hang you both——"

Dobbs groaned, and began to apostro-
phise his Maker.

"What should I do if I was Dobbs is to
take bull by horns—not delay a second—
taking up the Government offer of Reward
and Free Pardon, not being the actual
murderer—I, Septimus Dobbs, should confess to Spelter, and claim the Reward and
the Free Pardon."

"But you said Scruton was in custody?"
said Dobbs, in a hoarse whisper.

" Practically."

" In fact you said ?"

" Brackenbury is in charge of two of my men—so far as I am concerned he is in custody, though he does not know it—my men wait the signal to save your neck, and thus honourably earn all the money you have paid me—I am ready to arrest him on your confession."

" Oh ! my God ! oh ! my offended Maker, what shall I do ?" exclaimed Dobbs. " Give me time, Spelter; time to think, my dear friend !"

" Take a little more brandy," said Spelter, keeping down his own exultation; for, though his case was strong against Dobbs, he had invented some of the keenest of the blows he had struck in his imaginary brief.

It might be objected against Spelter's action that, as a police officer, he had no

right to lead Dobbs into a trap; indeed,
that he committed a breach of police law
in doing so; but Spelter had not obtained
his great reputation by over-scrupulous-
ness in such matters; and officers in his
position were allowed a wider latitude of
discretion seventy years ago than now;
and crime was of a more daring and
romantic character than it is now, in so
far as regards offences that were committed against the person.

"How easily a poor devil may be hanged
when he is innocent you already know,"
said Spelter, while Dobbs was thinking out
the points which had gone so straight home
to him. "Scruton presumed on that—
but Scruton has lived a good deal abroad,
and that's against him in many ways—only
discovered four and twenty hours ago last
piece of evidence against Short—Scruton's
marked guineas—buried with other crimin-

ating things beneath his bed-room floor—
if Short hadn't been killed I should have
hanged him."

" Oh ! Mr. Spelter, my dear friend,
what shall I do ?" said Dobbs, utterly
broken down and bewildered ; " you must
give me time."

"Ten minutes," was Spelter's reply—
" ten minutes—you'll never see the case
in a clearer light if you think about it
for a week."

" I will go into the next room," said
Dobbs, struggling to his feet.

" No, don't do that—better think it out
here—do you want anything ?—here is the
placard announcing the Reward and Free
Pardon—you have no wife—no children—
no ties—you can travel—change your
name—have known three different men
who have done it—one confessed before
question could be raised as to privilege of

being allowed to turn King's evidence—
other two allowed to do so because evidence difficult without them; knew two men
who might have been living now in clover,
who offered to turn King's evidence when
it was too late—we didn't want their confession—they were two fools, and they
were hanged accordingly."

"Oh, what an awful position to be
in, Mr. Spelter! How can I say that
that miserable man committed the deed?
If I died this minute, I could not!
He is a bad, wicked, dangerous man, no
doubt."

"Ten minutes up," said Spelter, looking at his watch and rising to his feet.

"Well, and what are you going to do?"
asked Dobbs.

"Arrest you!"

"Merciful Saviour!" exclaimed Dobbs,
trembling in every limb.

" If I do so without your confession you must appeal to a higher authority than mine to turn King's evidence—if you give yourself up to me—prompted by the weight of your sin, say, being a religious man; and I can say that on your own information I charge Scruton and yourself —why, then the Free Pardon is settled— you won't want the reward—Spelter can claim that—when all is over your life and liberty are secure—decide!—time's up— 'pon my soul it is !"

" Life is sweet!" gasped Dobbs.

" While there's life there's hope !" said Spelter.

" And time for repentance ! Time to make your peace with your Maker. Time to live a new life and atone !"

" Just so—Dobbs's counsel gives good advice."

"Mr. Spelter," said Dobbs, rising, and steadying himself against the table.

"Excuse me, I'll take it down," said Spelter, laying his hand upon a sheet of paper and dipping a pen into the ink.

"I have a statement to make to you in your capacity as a constable in the service of the law and of His Majesty the King," went on Dobbs. "I have reason to believe that Philip Scruton, now Lord Ellerbie, murdered his uncle. I am anxious to clear my conscience of a load of iniquity in connection therewith, and I am led to make this confession by the remorse I feel at the arrest and peril of Oliver North; but more particularly by the King's gracious offer of a Free Pardon to any person implicated in the crime, and not being the actual perpetrator thereof."

"Well put—Dobbs's counsel knows his business—excuse me—want a witness to your signature — forgive me taking a liberty."

Spelter went to the door, unlocked it, and called "Mrs. Briddon," Dobbs's house-keeper.

"Not her—not Briddon!" exclaimed Dobbs.

"As you please," said Spelter, whistling a low, peculiar whistle, which was prompt-ly answered by the man who had been sent down to Chesterfield to inquire into the Jessie Burns business, and whom Spelter had kept in the neighbourhood.

"Friend of mine from London," said Spelter—"brought him so that we shouldn't be disturbed—Mathers, just witness Mr. Dobbs's signature."

Dobbs, after reading it, appended a much firmer signature to the statement written down by Spelter than might have been expected.

Upon which Spelter "charged" him in the usual form; and at sight of a pair of handcuffs which Mathers somewhat prematurely produced, Dobbs fell down in a fit, foamed at the mouth, gnashed his teeth, glared hideously, writhed, clutched his cravat, tore his vest, and presently lay still as death.

"You will remain with him," said Spelter; "he'll come round—shall not lock him up till to-morrow—will send a doctor and a constable—Mathers, you were in luck when they sent you down here—give him some brandy when he revives—he is your prisoner. Have you your barkers with you?"

"Yes, sir," answered Mathers.

"You'll not need them—he'll be gentle as a lamb—set to praying, no doubt—be kind to him—he's done us a service—not the sort that dies game, but a villain, mark you—a cat's-paw scoundrel, Mathers—I'll return to you soon—the constable shall bring the doctor."

CHAPTER VIII.

JUSTICE OPENS HER EYES AT LAST.

And strange tales there be locked in the heart of
every town, that he who bringeth the keys of Patience
and Inquiry may unlock—Romances of Love and War,
tragedies of Assize, that do comprehend both rich and
poor, the titled and the commoner.

Local History.

UPON the information of Mr. Spelter,
it was deemed advisable that a file
of soldiers should be sent for from
Sheffield. There was ample excuse for
the movement of troops in the Midlands;
for civic strife and sedition were rife in

many districts, and the constabulary organizations were of the feeblest character. The local magistracy feared that riotous demonstrations might be made against Mr. Dobbs; and even a rescue of Oliver North attempted, so strong a feeling was growing up in his favour and against the persons who had brought about his arrest. The discovery of the marked guineas stolen from Scruton, and for which poor Marks had innocently suffered, re-opened that dreadful story, and the populace mixed it up with the present attempt to strain the law against another young fellow whose pluck and distinction had made him popular.

The troops came into Chesterfield during the night, and when the Scarsdale town woke up in the morning they were in charge of the House of Correction; they guarded the office of the county magistrate, before whom Oliver North was charged; they were in possession of Brackenbury Towers; they were posted in front of Dobbs's house in Glueman Gate; and the chief persons of the town said the magistracy had done right in claiming this timely provision against a breach of the peace.

The little office of the county magistrate was surrounded with a crowd that became intensely excited when a carriage drove up containing Lord Ellerbie, who, as he stepped out, guarded by two constables, was greeted with groans and hisses. Mr. Septimus Dobbs was similarly received. The populace did not know at that time of the change which had taken place in their relationship to the case which was exciting so much local feeling. It was soon, how-ever, buzzed about that Dobbs was in trouble; and when a messenger, coming

out of the magistrate's office, told the
crowd that Scruton himself was in custody,
a cheer was set up that compelled the
magistrate to pause in some sympathetic
observations he was making to Captain
North. But, if the crowd was surprised
by the scraps of intelligence that filtered
out of the court through messengers
and others, the chief astonishment was
reserved for Scruton himself. He had
affected to treat his arrest with contempt. He had even threatened the officers with condign punishment ; but when
Septimus Dobbs stood forward, pale and
haggard, to declare his confederacy, and
to offer his depositions as King's evidence,
the murderer's face fell, and the next moment he looked as if he would leap upon
Dobbs and strangle him. Dobbs shrank
back, inwardly offering up thanks that he

was a prisoner under the protection of the Court.

The magistrate was occupied the whole of the day in taking evidence ; and at the close considered he had heard sufficient to commit Philip Scruton, Earl of Ellerbie, and to hold Dobbs in custody pending the trial. The magistrate was anxious to rid the town of the responsibility of two such notable prisoners. By the advice of his clerk he concluded to commit them on the evidence of three witnesses, so that they might forthwith be conveyed to Derby.

Oliver North was discharged and bound over to give evidence against the prisoners. Upwards of two thousand people escorted him to the Hall in Lordsmill Street, where he was received by Susan, who fell into his arms, sobbing with joy. Mary Bertram was there, and her husband. At night tar-barrels were rolled about the town; a band of music paraded the streets; and a torchlight procession followed the prisoners on the road to Derby, singing some mad kind of ditty which Tom Bertram had set to what he called "The Rogue's March."

The next day all the leading townspeople called upon Oliver North at his lodgings to sympathise with him and congratulate him upon the quick proof of his innocence. Prominent among these were the Vicar and Mrs. Wingfield, Major George Wingfield, and Mrs. Major Wingfield. Besides these friends, there came Mr. and Mrs. Kirk, Father Busby, and a crowd of far more distinguished persons, with whom, however, this particular history is not concerned.

On the way to the gaol at Derby,

when the vigilance of the constables was relaxed, Scruton, ironed as he was, suddenly flung himself upon his fellow-prisoner Dobbs, striking him in the face with his manacled hands.

As the officers dragged him from his prostrate and bleeding victim, Scruton uttered a fierce threat against his life. "I'll kill you! you cur, before I die!" he hissed in the ear of his terrified confederate.

The murderous resolve cost him his own life.

It seemed as if he entered the gaol with that one motive of revenge fixed in his mind. From the first moment that he set foot within the prison he began to scheme, not an escape, but a means of obtaining access to Dobbs's cell. The prison was new, and indeed hardly finished in parts.

Scruton had not been in the place a month before he had obtained a plan of the prison from a gaol-bird whose friendship he had made during the exercising and other regulations which brought the prisoners into each other's company.   He had learnt from the chaplain the number and position of Dobbs's cell, and it troubled him sorely and excited his passion of revenge to know that the lawyer was receiving more considerate treatment than himself ; that he had long interviews daily with the persons who were getting up the case for the prosecution.

Scruton was committed to the March Assizes, so that he had a good deal of time on his hands, and he obtained some privileges and consideration not only on account of his rank, but by reason of his peculiarly mild behaviour since his incarceration. Once a week he had a visit from the lawyer whom he was instructing for his defence ; and the solicitor went away always telling the officer he was certain to prove the innocence of his client.

The lawyer in question was attended by a clerk who used to fee the turnkeys and others very liberally, on behalf of the prisoner, which was not forgotten by them in their views of gaol discipline as it affected Lord Ellerbie. The result was that on Christmas Eve, when the officers of the gaol were more than usually indulgent both to themselves and the prisoners under their charge, Scruton was creeping along the corridor beneath which Dobbs's cell was situated, a fac-simile key in one hand, his leg-irons in the other, and in his heart a palpitating, burning desire to beat Dobbs to death, when suddenly he came to a barrier which seemed like a door

that yielded to pressure. This was the sum-
mit of an unfinished flight of steps, intended
as a double communication to the upper corridor or third story cell, above which Scruton
had been confined, and which had only been
recently commenced. The barrier, instead
of being a door, was made of some loose
planks, upon which was printed a notice—
" Dangerous !   No Road !"   But it was
dark, and Scruton had had no intimation
of a second flight of stairs. An opening
had been made for the steps, and meanwhile in their place a ladder was left for
the convenience of masons working in the
adjacent right wing of the prison, which in
the daytime generally resounded with the
clink of the bricklayer's trowel.

All was still enough on this Christmas
Eve. There was a distant sound of bells,
it is true. Upon some minds the music
would have made a tender and sentimental

impression; but they did not touch Philip Scruton, for whom, however, it must be said that he had no particular memories of Christmas and its associations, his life having been chiefly spent in foreign lands, and never in the society of good women and worthy men.

"Curse it! where am I?" he muttered. "This must be the west end flight of steps marked on the plan, and the fool forgot to put in the door."

He pressed against the barrier with his shoulder. His legs were still partially shackled, which made his movements difficult; though he had no doubt about his physical capacity to do all he wished when he was inside the cell where Dobbs had been trying to persuade himself and his keepers of the sincerity of his penitence by singing a Christmas hymn. He little thought how near to him was his mortal foe, a bar of iron in his hand, a bitter, bloody resolve of murder in his heart,

"It yields," muttered Scruton—"a door they don't lock, that's the reason it is not marked, I suppose. There is a light in the corridor below, always. Once there, I am right."

He pressed against the barrier.

"Ah! I see a glimmer of the lamp," he muttered.

It was a lantern hung over some building *débris* which the workmen had left near the ladder by a passage leading to the night-warder's room.

"Yes, that's the light!" he said, re-assured, "and the place as still as Septimus Dobbs will be before these cursed bells have done ringing. So open, curse you!" he said, in a hoarse whisper, "open, damn you!" He pressed his whole weight against the yield-

ing plank, and away went the barrier,
Scruton with it, headlong to the pavement
of the first floor.   Struck by timbers as he
fell, he uttered but one stifled groan; and
when the warders on guard rushed to the
spot they found the mangled body of Scruton, the face crushed out of all shape, a
hideous spectacle of death.

The general verdict of Chesterfield and
the county was that he had cheated the
scaffold; while the people of Grassmoor,
the peasants around Brackenbury, and the
old servants of the late Earl, said he had
fulfilled the awful destiny of his house;
and the Vicar of Chesterfield, "improving
the occasion" in a sermon, showed that even
from a worldly point of view justice had
overtaken the criminal at a peculiarly fitting
moment, for he had been allowed to taste
the sweets of power and gold only to have
the longed-for and ill-gotten gains snatch-

ed from him at the moment of his guilty
enjoyment of them.

It was a solemn service that of the old
parish church, and the people were rejoiced to see the Countess of Ellerbie
enter the sacred precincts, walk up the
old aisle, and, leaning on Major Wingfield's
arm, take her place in the Vicar's pew.
Captain North followed with old Mrs.
Wingfield, and Mrs. Wingfield the younger
was escorted by a London visitor, an old
gentleman in a brown velvet suit with a
tie-wig, the good old style of their grand-
fathers. Mrs. Goodenough, a Quaker-like
old lady, leading a pretty little boy, followed. Mr. Hardwick was not present.
He had become a devout Catholic, and
could only worship at Brackenbury Towers.
Perhaps this had influenced Susan, as much
as Oliver's arguments, in her return to the
old church, where on this very day, when

the Vicar preached from the text, "Ven-
geance is Mine, saith the Lord," he read
"for the first time of asking" the banns of
marriage between Oliver North and Susan,
Countess of Ellerbie.

CHAPTER IX.

SUMMER COMES AGAIN.

Conquer we shall, but we must first contend ;
'Tis not the fight that crowns us, but the end.

HERRICK.

BUT the Countess gave Brackenbury Towers to Father Busby and his Church, with the gardens and lake; and to this day the monastery in the valley below Grassmoor is a place of religious rest and peace; an institution at first somewhat resented by the people, who had no liking for what they called "a hot-bed of priests in the neighbourhood," but

in due course the meekness and charity of
the brotherhood won their way to local sympathy, and the monastery of Brackenbury,
with its legends, its solemn services, and
its shrine, is now a sort of sleeping mystery among the Derbyshire oaks which
only strangers and tourists seem to trouble
about.

It was generally felt that the gift was
a strange one on the part of the Countess; but she was herself a strange person, and, moreover, old Hardwick had
thrown in his lot with Brackenbury, and
was permitted to occupy the old Earl's
suite of rooms, and to have the library all
to himself.   It had cost her many a pang,
but Susan had never spoken to the old
man since he had crowned the edifice of
his conspiracies against her with the proposition that she should become Scruton's
wife.

Not alone in the monastery of Brackenbury are the tourists of Derbyshire interested.   They hunt among the gravestones
of the little churchyard of Grassmoor for
the memorial of Jacob Marks, whose mar-
tyred remains were removed by Government authority from the gaol at Derby to
be interred at Grassmoor with solemn
Christian burial.   Fresh flowers used to
be continually laid upon the piled-up mound
of earth which the simple headstone marks.
The village of Grassmoor regarded it as a
great boon to have the poor youth at rest
among the family dead, side by side with
the villagers whom he knew.   It was a
sort of recompense to them for an awful
miscarriage of justice, and also for a libel
on the honour and honesty of the village.
Farmer Kirk regarded the grave and headstone with a melancholy kind of triumph;
for while the epitaph set forth the virtues

of Jacob Marks it blasted for all time the
memory of the lad's cruel betrayer. Once
a year Mary and Tom made a point of
dressing in their best, with a bit of added
crape, and going to the Grassmoor churchyard as on a pilgrimage, and they recalled
the past on that sad festival of their
friend's death. In the interval everybody
seemed to put flowers on the grave, the
Kirk children and the Bertram children,
and the young and old of the little Derbyshire village, a grassy spot now being
rapidly changed, I fear, into a busy scene
of coal-getting and iron-smelting; yet still
possessing old-time glimpses of undulating
meadow-lands, old-fashioned flower-gardens,
dreamy bits of coppice, and English lanes
ragged with trailing hedgerows and moss-
grown foot-paths.

Five years after the Vicar published the
banns of marriage between Oliver North

and Susan, Countess of Ellerbie, one summer day there sat under the group of elms
in front of the old Hall of the Hard-
wicks, the residence of Captain Oliver
North, a notable party of old friends
gathered together at the christening of
Susan's third son. It was her own wish
that they should drink tea on the lawn.
There were Mrs. Bertram, and her five-
year-old Tom, a sturdy little yeoman; the
Sergeant-Major, now a prosperous farmer
at Stoney Hollow, with his own freehold, a
birthday present to Mary from the owner
thereof; Mr. and Mrs. Kirk, white-haired
both, but apple-cheeked and ruddy with
health; all the Wingfields, little George,
the admiration of everybody, and Jessie
his mother, as lovely and charming a little
lady as the county could produce. Oliver
North, while his face beamed with love
and happiness over all, was listening, not

to the voices of the company, with its united story of love and trouble mingling in the reminiscences of his own life, but to the distant music of the mill, wafted from the adjacent meadows on the summer breeze, which was singing to him its song of triumph; for not only on the Derwent near Derby had he won that battle he talked of on the eve of Vitoria, but here in Chesterfield, where they had broken his models and driven him forth with curses and groans a dozen years before.

The tea and sugar for that little party on the lawn was supplied from the well-known store of Richard Holmes, whose business had flourished immensely from the day he married Susan Jane. It would be to inquire too curiously to trace the sugar to so bitter a source as the plantation of Septimus Dobbs; but that arrant scoundrel had found his way to Jamaica as the partner of a sugar-planter, a widow whose husband had been his client.

It is not in history that the wicked have always been punished in this world; nor is it possible for the novelist, even taking some pardonable liberties with the concerns of the persons whose lives he narrates, to control the destinies of all his subjects. Lawyer Dobbs was the sort of man to fight his way through difficulties, dangers, and crimes of all kinds and degrees, crawling where he could not walk, creeping where he could not climb, fawning where he could not bully, cringeing where he could not strike, praying when he wished to impress men rather than God, and in short trimming his sails to suit every breeze, and ballasting his hollow heart to suit every sea. Perhaps that Jamaica widow was a very wicked, bad woman, and God sent her Dobbs for a husband. The wretch must have had his use, or he would not have come into the world. There is no knowing what frightful deeds the Jamaica widow had been guilty of to have Dobbs for a punishment.

On that summer night, when the old friends had all gone home, Oliver and Susan wandered arm in arm through the Hall garden, past the now silent mill, and among the hay, to that spot where first she confessed her love when the bands were playing the wild promise, " We will return safe back again to the girls we leave behind us." And Oliver (who had already changed the aspect of manufactures in the Midlands and in the north), as they walked home again through the sweet-smelling meadows, told his wife a fairy-tale of invention which is coming true.

"One day, Susan," he said, "our dear little chap whom you *would* call Oliver will walk in these meadows with a friend. He will hear that mill, all dark as it is, humming its busy music. While he is talking of his good and beautiful mother, he will tell his friend how she encouraged his father to persevere in his work of invention. Then he will open the door and strike a light; and he will show his guest a mill going by itself, a mill at work alone in the darkness, untended, the revolving machines depositing their yarn, and at a later day even their woven goods ready to be gathered and packed the next morning. Even that will not be more wonderful than the carrying of merchandise to Liverpool in a steam-coach and despatching it over the sea in a ship without sails; and that is of our time. The untended mill, the dreamy power at work all alone in the night, singing its song in chorus with the brook and the breezes of heaven : *that* is the legacy we leave to our son !"

He paused to kiss her wondering face.

" I cannot look so far into the future," she said ; " would that the present could last for ever !"

" My darling !" he exclaimed, as he pressed her to his heart.

" There is no invention," she said, " so beautiful as Love !"

THE END.

LONDON: PRINTED BY DUNCAN MACDONALD, BLENHEIM HOUSE.

MESSRS. HURST AND BLACKETT'S
LIST OF NEW WORKS.

ROYAL WINDSOR. By W. HEPWORTH DIXON.
Second Edition. Volumes I. and II. Demy 8vo. 30s.

CONTENTS OF VOLS. I. AND II.—Castle Hill, Norman Keep, First King's House, Lion Heart, Kingless Windsor, Windsor Won, Geoffrey Plantagenet, Windsor Lost, The Fallen Deputy, The Queen Mother, Maud de Braose, The Barons' War, Second King's House, Edward of Carnarvon, Perot de Gaveston, Isabel de France, Edward of Windsor, Crecy, Patron Saints. St. George, Society of St. George, Lady Salisbury, David King of Scots, Third King's House, Ballad Windsor, The Fair Countess, Richard of Bordeaux, Court Parties, Royal Favourites, Rehearsing for Windsor, In the Great Hall, Simon de Burley, Radcote Bridge, A Feast of Death, Geoffrey Chaucer, At Winchester Tower, St. George's Chapel, The Little Queen, At Windsor, Duchess Philippote, The Windsor Plot, Bolingbroke, Court of Chivalry, Wager of Battle, Captive Little Queen, A New Year's Plot, Night of the Kings, Dona Juana, Constance of York, The Norman Tower, The Legal Heir, Prince Hal, The Devil's Tower, In Captivity Captive, Attempt at Rescue, Agincourt, Kaiser Sigismund, The Witch Queen, Sweet Kate, The Maid of Honour, Lady Jane, Henry of Windsor, Richard of York, Two Duchesses, York and Lancaster, Union of the Roses.

"'Royal Windsor' follows in the same lines as 'Her Majesty's Tower,' and aims at weaving a series of popular sketches of striking events which centre round Windsor Castle. Mr. Dixon makes everything vivid and picturesque. Those who liked 'Her Majesty's Tower' will find these volumes equally pleasant reading."—*Athenæum.*

"A truly fine and interesting book. It is a valuable contribution to English history; worthy of Mr. Dixon's fame, worthy of its grand subject."—*Morning Post.*

"Mr. Dixon has supplied us with a highly entertaining book. 'Royal Windsor' is eminently a popular work, bristling with anecdotes and amusing sketches of historical characters. It is carefully written, and is exceedingly pleasant reading. The story is brightly told; not a dull page can be found. Mr. Dixon is to be congratulated on having put so much information into so agreeable a shape."—*Examiner.*

"These volumes will find favour with the widest circle of readers. From the first days of Norman Windsor to the Plantagenet period Mr. Dixon tells the story of this famous castle in his own picturesque, bright, and vigorous way."—*Daily Telegraph.*

"Mr. Hepworth Dixon has found a congenial subject in 'Royal Windsor.' Under the sanction of the Queen, he has enjoyed exceptional opportunities of most searching and complete investigation of the Royal House and every other part of Windsor Castle, in and out, above ground and below ground."—*Daily News.*

VOLS. III. AND IV. OF ROYAL WINDSOR. By W. HEPWORTH DIXON. Demy 8vo. 30s. Completing the Work.

CONTENTS OF VOLS. III. AND IV.—St. George's Hall, The Tudor Tower, A Windsor Comedy, The Secret Room, Treaties of Windsor, The Private Stair, Disgrading a Knight, In a King's House, The Maiden's Tower, Black Days, The Virgin Bride, Elegy on Windsor, Fair Geraldine, Course of Song, A Windsor Gospeller, Windsor Martyrs, A Royal Reference, Hatchment Down, The People's Friend, St. George's Enemy, Lady Elizabeth's Grace, Queen Mary, Grand Master of St. George, Deanery and Dean, Sister Temperance, Elizabeth's Lovers, Dudley Constable, The Schoolmaster, Peace, Proclaimed, Shakespere's Windsor, The Two Shakesperes, The Merry Wives, Good Queen Bess, House of Stuart, The Little Park, The Queen's Court, The King's Knights, Spurious Peace, King Christian, A Catholic Dean, Apostasy, Expulsion, Forest Rights, Book of Sports, Windsor Cross, In the Forest, Windsor Seized, Under the Keep, At Bay, Feudal Church, Parleying, Roundheads, Cavalier Prisoners, Head-Quarters, The New Model, Last Days of Royalty, Saints in Council, Changing Sides, Bagshot Lodge, At Length, Cutting Down, Windsor Uncrowned, A "Merry" Cæsar, Windsor Catholic, The Catastrophe, Domestic Life, Home.

1

MESSRS. HURST AND BLACKETT'S
NEW WORKS—*Continued.*

DIARY OF A TOUR IN SWEDEN, NORWAY,
AND RUSSIA, IN 1827. By THE MARCHIONESS OF WESTMINSTER. 1 vol. Demy 8vo. 15s.

"A bright and lively record So pleasantly are the letters written which Lady Westminster sent home, so full are they of the enthusiasm and good humour which enabled her to appreciate the sunny, and endure the cloudy, side of her wanderings, that her book is most agreeable; and it has this special merit, that it brings clearly before us a number of the great people of former days, royal and imperial personages, whose intimate acquaintance the traveller's rank enabled her to make."—*Athenæum.*

"A very agreeable and instructive volume."—*Saturday Review.*

"We recommend Lady Westminster's diary to all classes of readers as a highly instructive book of interesting travel, replete with graphic sketches of social life and scenery, and abounding in many entertaining anecdotes. It is written throughout with excellent taste and good sense."—*Court Journal.*

HOLIDAYS IN EASTERN FRANCE; Sketches
of Travel in CHAMPAGNE, FRANCHE-COMTE, the JURA, the VALLEY of the DOUBS, &c. By M. BETHAM-EDWARDS, Author of "A Winter with the Swallows," &c. 1 vol. 8vo. With Illustrations. 15s.

"Miss Edwards passed her holidays last summer in visiting a singularly interesting and beautiful country. Her present volume, written in the same pleasant style as that which described her wanderings in Western France, is so much the more to be recommended that its contents are fresher and more novel."—*Saturday Review.*

"Readers of this work will find plenty of fresh information about some of the most delightful parts of France. The descriptions of scenery are as graphic as the sketches of character are lifelike."—*Globe.*

"The tourist could not have a pleasanter companion than this pretty book, and its well laid out itineraries."—*Graphic.*

THE YOUTH OF QUEEN ELIZABETH. Edited,
from the French of L. WIESENER, by CHARLOTTE M. YONGE, Author of "The Heir of Redclyffe," &c. 2 vols. crown 8vo. 21s.

"M. Wiesener is to be complimented on the completeness, accuracy, and research shown in this work. He has drawn largely on the French Archives, the Public Record Office, and British Museum, for information contained in original documents, to some of which notice is directed for the first time. M. Wiesener's work is well worth translating, for it is most interesting as showing the education and circumstances which tended to form the character of that extraordinary queen. Miss Yonge appears to have successfully accomplished the task which she has undertaken."—*Athenæum.*

"An excellent and interesting book. M. Wiesener has worked conscientiously and carefully from original sources."—*Academy.*

RORAIMA AND BRITISH GUIANA, with a
Glance at Bermuda, the West Indies, and the Spanish Main. By J. W. BODDAM-WHETHAM. 8vo. With Map and Illustrations. 15s.

"The author has succeeded in producing an interesting and readable book of travels. His remarks on every-day life in the tropics, his notes on the geography and natural history of the countries he visited, and, above all, his vivid descriptions of scenery, combine to form a record of adventure which in attractiveness it will not be easy to surpass."—*Athenæum.*

"Mr. Whetham writes with vigour, and describes the life in the forests and on the rivers and prairies of South America with a picturesqueness and freshness of interest not inferior to that of the late Mr. Waterton's immortal wanderings. Mr. Whetham travelled in portions of Guiana little known, meeting with many adventures, seeing many strange sights, and taking notes which have furnished matter for a book of fascinating interest."—*Daily News.*

MESSRS. HURST AND BLACKETT'S
NEW WORKS—*Continued.*

CONVERSATIONS WITH DISTINGUISHED PERSONS
during the Second Empire, from 1860 to 1863. By the Late
NASSAU W. SENIOR. Edited by his Daughter, M. C. M. SIMPSON.
2 vols. 8vo. 30s.

Among other persons whose conversations are given in these volumes are:—Prince
Napoleon; the Duc de Broglie; the Marquises Chambrun, Lasteyrie, Palla-
vicini, Vogué; Marshal Randon; Counts Arrivabene, Circourt, Corcelle, Ker-
gorlay, Montalembert, Rémusat, Zamoyski; Generals Changarnier, Fénélon,
Trochu; Lords Cowley and Clyde; Sir W. Erle; Messieurs Ampère, Beau-
mont, Chambol, Chevalier, Cousin, Dayton, Drouyn de Lhuys, Duchâtel, Du-
faure, Dumon, Duvergier de Hauranne, Guizot, Haldimand, Hotze, Lamartine,
Loménie, Lavergne, Lanjuinais, Maury, Marochetti, Masson, Mérimée, Mohl,
Odillon Barrot, Pelletan, Pietri, Rénan, St. Hilaire, Slidell, Thiers, De Witt;
Mesdames Circourt, Cornu, Mohl, &c.

"Mr. Senior's **Conversations with M. Thiers, M. Guizot,** &c., published about a
year and a half ago, were **the most** interesting volumes of the **series which had**
appeared up to that time, and these new 'Conversations' are **hardly, if at all, less**
welcome and important. A large part of this delightful book is **made up of studies**
by various critics, from divers points of view, of the character **of Louis Napoleon,**
and of more or less vivid and accurate explanations of his **tortuous policy.** The
work contains a few extremely interesting reports of **conversations with M. Thiers.**
There are some valuable reminiscences of Lamartine, **and among men of a some-**
what later day, of Prince Napoleon, **Drouyn de Lhuys, Montalembert, Victor**
Cousin, Rénan, and the Chevaliers."—*Athenæum.*

CONVERSATIONS WITH M. THIERS, M. GUIZOT,
and other Distinguished Persons, during the Second Empire. By
the Late NASSAU W. SENIOR. Edited by his Daughter, M. C. M.
SIMPSON. 2 vols. demy 8vo. 30s.

Among other persons whose conversations are recorded in these volumes are:—
King Leopold; the Duc de Broglie; Lord Cowley; Counts Arrivabene, Cor-
celle, Daru, Flahault, Kergolay, Montalembert; Generals Lamoricière and
Chrzanowski; Sir Henry Ellis; Messieurs Ampère, Beaumont, Blanchard,
Bouffet, Auguste Chevalier, Victor Cousin, De Witt, Duchâtel, Ducpetiaux,
Dumon, Dussard, Duvergier de Hauranne, Léon Faucher, Frère-Orban, Grim-
blot, Guizot, Lafitte, Labaume, Lamartine, Lanjuinais, Mallac, Manin, Mérimée,
Mignet, Jules Mohl, Montanelli, Odillon-Barrot, Quêtelet, Rémusat, Rogier,
Rivet, Rossini, Horace Say. Thiers, Trouvé-Chauvel, Villemain, Wolowski;
Mesdames Circourt, Cornu, Ristori, &c.

"This new series of Mr. Senior's 'Conversations' has been for some years past
known in manuscript to his more intimate friends, and it has always been felt that
no former series would prove **more** valuable or important. Mr. Senior had a social
position which gave him admission into the best literary and political circles of
Paris. He was a cultivated and sensible man, who knew how to take full advantage of such an opening. And above all, he had by long practice so trained his
memory as to enable it to recall all the substance, and often the words, of the long
conversations which he was always holding. These conversations he wrote down
with a surprising accuracy, and then handed the manuscript to his friends, that
they might correct or modify his report of what they had said. This book thus
contains the opinions of eminent men given in the freedom of conversation, and
afterwards carefully revised. Of their value there cannot be a question. The book
is one of permanent historical interest. There is scarcely a page without some
memorable statement by some memorable man. Politics and society and literature
—the three great interests that make up life—are all discussed in turn, and there is
no discussion which is unproductive of weighty thought or striking fact."—*Athenæum.*

"The present selection of Mr. Senior's Journals, edited with remarkable skill
and judgment by Mrs. Simpson, is extraordinarily full and interesting. Although
the unreserved and original communications of Thiers are especially fascinating,
the book would be abundantly interesting if it consisted only of the reports of
conversations with Guizot, Montalembert, Cousin, Lamartine, and other persons of
celebrity and eminence."—*Saturday Review.*

MESSRS. HURST AND BLACKETT'S
NEW WORKS—*Continued.*

HISTORY OF TWO QUEENS : CATHARINE
OF ARAGON and ANNE BOLEYN. By W. HEPWORTH DIXON.
Second Edition. Vols. 1 & 2. Demy 8vo. 30s.

"In two handsome volumes Mr. Dixon here gives us the first instalment of a new historical work on a most attractive subject. The book is in many respects a favourable specimen of Mr. Dixon's powers. It is the most painstaking and elaborate that he has yet written. . . . . On the whole, we may say that the book is one which will sustain the reputation of its author as a writer of great power and versatility, that it gives a new aspect to many an old subject, and presents in a very striking light some of the most recent discoveries in English history."—*Athenæum.*

"In these volumes the author exhibits in a signal manner his special powers and finest endowments. It is obvious that the historian has been at especial pains to justify his reputation, to strengthen his hold upon the learned, and also to extend his sway over the many who prize an attractive style and interesting narrative more highly than laborious research and philosophic insight."—*Morning Post.*

"The thanks of all students of English history are due to Mr. Hepworth Dixon for his clever and original work, 'History of two Queens.' The book is a valuable contribution to English history. The author has consulted a number of original sources of information—in particular the archives at Simancas, Alcala, and Venice. Mr. Dixon is a skilful writer. His style, singularly vivid, graphic, and dramatic—is alive with human and artistic interest. Some of the incidental descriptions reach a very high level of picturesque power."—*Daily News.*

VOLS. III. & IV. OF THE HISTORY OF TWO
QUEENS: CATHARINE OF ARAGON and ANNE BOLEYN.
By W. HEPWORTH DIXON. *Second Edition.* Demy 8vo. Price 30s.
Completing the Work.

"These concluding volumes of Mr. Dixon's 'History of two Queens' will be perused with keen interest by thousands of readers. Whilst no less valuable to the student, they will be far more enthralling to the general reader than the earlier half of the history. Every page of what may be termed Anne Boleyn's story affords a happy illustration of the author's vivid and picturesque style. The work should be found in every library."—*Post.*

"Mr. Dixon has pre-eminently the art of interesting his readers. He has produced a narrative of considerable value, conceived in a spirit of fairness, and written with power and picturesque effect."—*Daily News.*

HISTORY OF WILLIAM PENN, Founder of
Pennsylvania. By W. HEPWORTH DIXON. A NEW LIBRARY EDITION.
1 vol. demy 8vo, with Portrait. 12s.

"Mr. Dixon's 'William Penn' is, perhaps, the best of his books. He has now revised and issued it with the addition of much fresh matter. It is now offered in a sumptuous volume, matching with Mr. Dixon's recent books, to a new generation of readers, who will thank Mr. Dixon for his interesting and instructive memoir of one of the worthies of England."—*Examiner.*

FREE RUSSIA. By W. HEPWORTH DIXON. *Third*
Edition. 2 vols. 8vo, with Coloured Illustrations. 30s.

"Mr. Dixon's book will be certain not only to interest but to please its readers and it deserves to do so. It contains a great deal that is worthy of attention, and is likely to produce a very useful effect."—*Saturday Review.*

THE SWITZERS. By W. HEPWORTH DIXON.
Third Edition. 1 vol. demy 8vo. 15s.

"A lively, interesting, and altogether novel book on Switzerland. It is full of valuable information on social, political, and ecclesiastical questions, and, like all Mr. Dixon's books, is eminently readable."—*Daily News.*

4

MESSRS. HURST AND BLACKETT'S
NEW WORKS—*Continued.*

MEMOIRS OF GEORGIANA, LADY CHATTER-
TON; With some Passages from her Diary. By E. HENEAGE DERING. 1 vol. demy 8vo. 15s.

Among other persons mentioned in this work are Lords Lansdowne, Brougham, Macaulay, Lytton, Houghton; Messrs. Wilberforce, Wordsworth, Hallam, Rogers, Moore, Sydney Smith, Landor, Lockhart, Fonblanque, Warburton, Harness, Chantrey; Count Montalembert, Dr. Ullathorne, Dr. Newman, Joanna Baillie, Lady Gifford, Lady Cork, Mrs. Somerville, Mrs. Norton, &c.

"Lady Chatterton's Diary gives a sketch of society during a well known but ever-interesting period. Mr. Dering may be congratulated on having furnished a graceful epilogue to the story of an interesting life."—*Athenæum.*

"In this work we have the pleasant picture of a literary artist and an amiable lady, and some interesting anecdotes which give value to the volume."—*John Bull.*

A LEGACY: Being the Life and Remains of JOHN
MARTIN, Schoolmaster and Poet. Written and Edited by the Author of "JOHN HALIFAX." 2 vols. crown 8vo. With Portrait. 21s.

"This is, in many respects, a remarkable book. It records the life, work, aspirations, and death of a schoolmaster and poet, of lowly birth but high-strung and ambitious soul. His writings brim with vivid thought, keen analysis of feeling, touches of poetic sentiment, and trenchant criticism of men and books, expressed in scholarly language."—*Guardian.*

"Mrs. Craik has related a beautiful and pathetic story—a story of faith and courage and untiring energy on the part of a young and gifted man, who might under other circumstances have won a place in literature. The story is one worth reading."—*Pall Mall Gazette.*

"In these volumes a well-known novelist presents us with a history so touching, so marvellous, and so simple, as no invention could produce. Few more pathetic or more instructive volumes have fallen in our way."—*Morning Post.*

LONDONIANA. By EDWARD WALFORD, M.A.,
Author of "The County Families," &c. 2 volumes crown 8vo. 21s.

"A highly interesting and entertaining book. It bristles with anecdotes and amusing sketches. The style is vivid, graphic, and dramatic, and the descriptions are given with a terseness and vigour that rivet the attention of the reader. The historian, the antiquarian, and the lover of romance will combine in pronouncing 'Londoniana' one of the most readable books of the day."—*Court Journal.*

"There is variety and amusement in Mr. Walford's volumes."—*Pall Mall Gazette.*

"These volumes are interesting and entertaining."—*John Bull.*

THE THEATRE FRANCAIS IN THE REIGN
OF LOUIS XV. By ALEXANDER BAILLIE COCHRANE, M.P. 1 vol. demy 8vo. 15s.

"A most valuable contribution to dramatic literature. All members of the profession should read it."—*Morning Post.*

"In this handsome volume Mr. Cochrane gives us a new work on a most attractive subject, which will be perused with keen interest by thousands of readers. It is written in a style singularly vivid, dramatic, and interesting. The variety of scenes described in this pleasant volume, the historical personages and dramatic artists crowded on the canvas, and the truthful account of the French stage, form an intellectual treat of the highest order. 'The Théâtre Français' will take its place among the best standard works of the day, and find its way into every well-selected library, fully sustaining the reputation of its skilful author."—*Court Journal.*

HISTORIC CHATEAUX: BLOIS, FONTAINEBLEAU,
VINCENNES. By ALEXANDER BAILLIE COCHRANE, M.P. 1 vol. 8vo. 15s.

"A very interesting volume."—*Times.*

"A lively and agreeable book, full of action and colour."—*Athenæum.*

"This book is bright, pleasant reading."—*British Quarterly Review.*

"A well executed book by a polished and vigorous writer."—*The World.*

MESSRS. HURST AND BLACKETT'S
NEW WORKS—*Continued.*

VOLS. I. & II. OF HER MAJESTY'S TOWER.
By W. HEPWORTH DIXON. DEDICATED BY EXPRESS PERMISSION TO THE QUEEN. *Sixth Edition.* 8vo. 30s.

FROM THE TIMES:—"All the civilized world—English, Continental, and American—takes an interest in the Tower of London. The Tower is the stage upon which has been enacted some of the grandest dramas and saddest tragedies in our national annals. If, in imagination, we take our stand on those time-worn walls, and let century after century flit past us, we shall see in due succession the majority of the most famous men and lovely women of England in the olden time. We shall see them jesting, jousting, love-making, plotting, and then anon, perhaps, commending their souls to God in the presence of a hideous masked figure, bearing an axe in his hands. It is such pictures as these that Mr. Dixon, with considerable skill as an historical limner, has set before us in these volumes. Mr. Dixon dashes off the scenes of Tower history with great spirit. His descriptions are given with such terseness and vigour that we should spoil them by any attempt at condensation. In conclusion, we may congratulate the author on this work. Both volumes are decidedly attractive, and throw much light on our national history."

VOLS. III. & IV. OF HER MAJESTY'S TOWER.
By W. HEPWORTH DIXON. DEDICATED BY EXPRESS PERMISSION TO THE QUEEN. Completing the Work. *Third Edition.* Demy 8vo. 30s.

ROUND THE WORLD IN SIX MONTHS. By
LIEUT.-COLONEL E. S. BRIDGES, Grenadier Guards. 1. vol 8vo. 15s.

"The author may be congratulated on his success, for his pages are light and pleasant. The volume will be found both amusing and useful."—*Athenæum.*

"Colonel Bridges' book has the merit of being lively and readable. His advice to future travellers as well as his estimate of expenses may be found serviceable."—*Pall Mall Gazette.*

"A thoroughly interesting and amusing book, as full of solid matter as pleasant anecdote. We have not met a truer picture of American, Japanese, Chinese, Indian, Egyptian, or Maltese scenery and surroundings."—*Court Journal.*

A YOUNG SQUIRE OF THE SEVENTEENTH
CENTURY, from the Papers of CHRISTOPHER JEAFFRESON, of Dullingham House, Cambridgeshire. Edited by JOHN CORDY JEAFFRESON, Author of "A Book about Doctors," &c. 2 vols. crown 8vo. 21s.

"Two volumes of very attractive matter:—letters which illustrate agriculture, commerce, war, love, and social manners, accounts of passing public events, and details which are not to be found in the Gazettes, and which come with singular freshness from private letters."—*Athenæum.*

"Two agreeable and important volumes. They deserve to be placed on library shelves with Pepys, Evelyn, and Reresby."—*Notes and Queries.*

THE SEA OF MOUNTAINS: AN ACCOUNT OF
LORD DUFFERIN'S TOUR THROUGH BRITISH COLUMBIA IN 1876. By MOLYNEUX ST. JOHN. 2 vols. crown 8vo. With Portrait of Lord Dufferin. 21s.

"Mr. St. John has given us in these pages a record of all that was seen and done in a very successful visit. His book is instructive, and it should be interesting to the general reader."—*Times.*

"Mr. St. John is a shrewd and lively writer. The reader will find ample variety in his book, which is well worth perusal."—*Pall Mall Gazette.*

"These volumes are amusing, interesting, and even valuable. They give us a very clear idea of the great quarrel between British Columbia and the Dominion of Canada; and they contain a full report of Lord Dufferin's great speech at Victoria. Then there are some graphic sketches of social life and scenery, and some entertaining stories."—*Spectator.*

MESSRS. HURST AND BLACKETT'S NEW WORKS—*Continued.*

CELEBRITIES I HAVE KNOWN. By LORD WILLIAM PITT LENNOX. *Second Series.* 2 volumes demy 8vo. 30s.

Among other persons mentioned in the Second Series of this work are—The Princess Charlotte and Prince Leopold; the Dukes of Wellington and Beaufort; the Earls of Durham and Carlisle; Lords Byron, Clyde, Adolphus Fitzclarence, and Cockburn; Sirs Walter Scott, G. Wombwell, A. Barnard, John Elley, Sidney, Harry, and C. F. Smith; Count D'Orsay; Dr. Dodd; Messrs. Thomas Moore, Theodore Hook, Leigh Hunt, Jerdan, James, Horace, and Albert Smith, Beazley, Tattersall, Hudson, Ude, George Colman, The Kembles, G. F. Cooke, Charles Young, Edmund and Charles Kean, Yates, Harley; Miss Foote; Mrs. Nisbet; Mesdames Catalani, Grassini, Rachel, &c.

"This new series of Lord William Lennox's reminiscences is fully as entertaining as the preceding one. Lord William makes good use of an excellent memory, and he writes easily and pleasantly."—*Pall Mall Gazette.*

"One of the best books of the season. Pleasant anecdotes, exciting episodes, smart sayings, witticisms, and repartees are to be found on every page."—*Court Journal.*

COACHING; With ANECDOTES OF THE ROAD. By LORD WILLIAM PITT LENNOX, Author of "Celebrities I have Known," &c. Dedicated to His Grace the DUKE OF BEAUFORT, K.G., President, and the Members of the Coaching Club. 1 vol. demy 8vo. 15s.

"Lord William's book is genial, discursive, and gossipy. We are indebted to the author's personal recollections for some lively stories, and pleasant sketches of some of the more famous dragsmen. Nor does Lord William by any means limit himself to the English roads, and English coaches. Bianconi's Irish cars, the continental diligences, with anecdotes of His Grace of Wellington, when Lord William was acting as his aide-de-camp during the occupation of Paris, with many other matters more or less germane to his subject, are all brought in more or less naturally. Altogether his volume, with the variety of its contents, will be found pleasant reading."—*Pall Mall Gazette.*

LIFE OF MOSCHELES; WITH SELECTIONS FROM HIS DIARIES AND CORRESPONDENCE. By HIS WIFE. 2 vols. large post 8vo, with Portrait. 24s.

"This life of Moscheles will be a valuable book of reference for the musical historian, for the contents extend over a period of threescore years, commencing with 1794, and ending at 1870. We need scarcely state that all the portions of Moscheles' diary which refer to his intercourse with Beethoven, Hummel, Weber, Czerny, Spontini, Rossini, Auber, Halévy, Schumann, Cherubini, Spohr, Mendelssohn, F David, Chopin, J. B. Cramer, Clementi, John Field, Habeneck, Hauptmann, Kalkbrenner, Kiesewetter, C. Klingemann, Lablache, Dragonetti, Sontag, Persiani, Malibran, Paganini, Rachel, Ronzi de Begnis, De Beriot, Ernst, Donzelli, Cinti-Damoreau, Chelard, Bochsa, Laporte, Charles Kemble, Paton (Mrs. Wood), Schröder-Devrient, Mrs. Siddons, Sir H. Bishop, Sir G. Smart, Standigl, Thalberg, Berlioz, Velluti, C. Young, Balfe, Braham, and many other artists of note in their time, will recall a flood of recollections. It was a delicate task for Madame Moscheles to select from the diaries in reference to living persons, but her extracts have been judiciously made. Moscheles writes fairly of what is called the 'Music of the Future' and its disciples, and his judgments on Herr Wagner, Dr. Liszt, Rubenstein, Dr. von Bülow, Litolff, &c., whether as composers or executants, are in a liberal spirit. He recognizes cheerfully the talents of our native artists, Sir Sterndale Bennett, Mr. Macfarren, Madame Arabella Goddard, Mr. John Barnett, Mr. Hullah, Mrs. Shaw, Mr. A. Sullivan, &c. The celebrities with whom Moscheles came in contact, include Sir Walter Scott, Sir Robert Peel, the late Duke of Cambridge, the Bunsens, Louis Philippe, Napoleon the Third, Humboldt, Henry Heine, Thomas More, Count Nesselrode, the Duchess of Orleans, Prof. Wolf, &c. Indeed, the two volumes are full of amusing anecdotes."—*Athenæum.*

7

MESSRS. HURST AND BLACKETT'S
NEW WORKS—*Continued.*

WORDS OF HOPE AND COMFORT TO THOSE IN SORROW.
Dedicated by Permission to THE QUEEN. *Fourth Edition.* 1 vol. small 4to, 5s. bound.

"These letters, the work of a pure and devout spirit, deserve to find many readers. They are greatly superior to the average of what is called religious literature."—*Athenæum.*

"The writer of the tenderly-conceived letters in this volume was Mrs. Julius Hare, a sister of Mr. Maurice. They are instinct with the devout submissiveness and fine sympathy which we associate with the name of Maurice; but in her there is added a winningness of tact, and sometimes, too, a directness of language, which we hardly find even in the brother. The letters were privately printed and circulated, and were found to be the source of much comfort, which they cannot fail to afford now to a wide circle. A sweetly-conceived memorial poem, bearing the well-known initials, 'E. H. P.', gives a very faithful outline of the life."—*British Quarterly Review.*

"This touching and most comforting work is dedicated to THE QUEEN, who took a gracious interest in its first appearance, when printed for private circulation, and found comfort in its pages, and has now commanded its publication, that the world in general may profit by it. A more practical and heart-stirring appeal to the afflicted we have never examined."—*Standard.*

A MAN OF OTHER DAYS: Recollections of the MARQUIS DE BEAUREGARD.
Edited, from the French, by CHARLOTTE M. YONGE, Author of "The Heir of Redclyffe," &c. 2 vols. 21s.

"M. Costa de Beauregard lived long enough to see the last years of the Monarchy, the Revolution, and the early promise of General Bonaparte. The opening chapters of the work introduce us to Paris society at the time when it was perhaps the most brilliant; and it is amusing to accompany our hero to Mme. Geoffrin's salon, where Marmontel, Rochefoucauld, Greuze, Diderot, and many others, discourse literature, art, and philosophy."—*Saturday Review.*

OUR BISHOPS AND DEANS. By the Rev. F. ARNOLD, B.A.,
late of Christ Church, Oxford. 2 vols. 8vo. 30s.

"This work is good in conception and cleverly executed, and as thoroughly honest and earnest as it is interesting and able."—*John Bull.*

LIFE OF THE RT. HON. SPENCER PERCEVAL;
Including His Correspondence. By His Grandson, SPENCER WALPOLE. 2 vols. 8vo. With Portrait. 30s.

"This biography will take rank, as a faithful reflection of the statesman and his period, as also for its philosophic, logical, and dramatic completeness."—*Post.*

MY YOUTH, BY SEA AND LAND, FROM 1809 TO 1816.
By CHARLES LOFTUS, formerly of the Royal Navy, late of the Coldstream Guards. 2 vols. crown 8vo. 21s.

"Major Loftus played the part allotted to him with honour and ability, and he relates the story of his sea life with spirit and vigour. Some of his sea stories are as laughable as anything in 'Peter Simple,' while many of his adventures on shore remind us of Charles Lever in his freshest days. During his sea life Major Loftus became acquainted with many distinguished persons. Besides the Duke of Wellington, the Prince Regent, and William IV., he was brought into personal relation with the allied Sovereigns, the Duc D'Angoulême, Lord William Bentinck, and Sir Hudson Lowe. A more genial, pleasant, wholesome book we have not often read."—*Standard.*

ACROSS CENTRAL AMERICA. By J. W. BODDAM-WHETHAM.
8vo. With Illustrations. 15s.

"Mr. Boddam-Whetham writes easily and agreeably."—*Pall Mall Gazette.*
"A bright and lively account of interesting travel."—*Globe.*

MESSRS. HURST AND BLACKETT'S
PUBLICATIONS—*Continued.*

HISTORY OF ENGLISH HUMOUR. By the Rev. A. G. L'Estrange, Author of "The Life of the Rev. W. Harness," &c. 2 vols. crown 8vo. 21s.

"This work contains a large and varied amount of information. It is impossible to give any idea of the wealth of anecdote and epigram in its pages, and for anything like a proper appreciation of its value we must refer our readers to the book itself."—*John Bull.*

MY YEAR IN AN INDIAN FORT. By Mrs. Guthrie. 2 vols. crown 8vo. With Illustrations. 21s.

"Written with intelligence and ability."—*Pall Mall Gazette.*

"A pleasantly written book. Those who know India, and those who do not, may read the work with pleasure and profit."—*Standard.*

RECOLLECTIONS of COLONEL DE GONNE-VILLE. Edited from the French by Charlotte M. Yonge, Author of the "Heir of Redclyffe," &c. 2 vols. crown 8vo. 21s.

"This work discloses a variety of details of interest connected with Napoleon's escape from Elba, the Hundred Days, the Bourbon Restoration, and the Revolution of July, 1830."—*The Times.*

THROUGH FRANCE AND BELGIUM, BY RIVER AND CANAL, IN THE STEAM YACHT "YTENE." By W. J. C. Moens, R.V.Y.C. 1 vol. 8vo. With Illustrations. 15s.

MY LIFE, FROM 1815 TO 1849. By Charles Loftus, formerly of the Royal Navy, late of the Coldstream Guards. Author of "My Youth by Sea and Land." 2 vols. crown 8vo. 21s.

"A thoroughly interesting and readable book."—*Standard.*

A BOOK ABOUT THE TABLE. By J. C. Jeaffreson. 2 vols. 8vo. 30s.

"This book is readable and amusing from first to last."—*Morning Post.*

COSITAS ESPANOLAS; OR, EVERY-DAY LIFE IN Spain. By Mrs. Harvey, of Ickwell-Bury, Author of "Turkish Harems and Circassian Homes." *Second Edition.* 1 vol. 8vo. 15s.

PEARLS OF THE PACIFIC. By J. W. Boddam-Whetham. 1 vol. Demy 8vo, with 8 Illustrations. 15s.

"The literary merits of this work are of a very high order."—*Athenæum.*

TURKISH HAREMS & CIRCASSIAN HOMES. By Mrs. Harvey, of Ickwell-Bury. 8vo. *Second Edition.* 15s.

MEMOIRS OF QUEEN HORTENSE, MOTHER OF NAPOLEON III. Cheaper Edition, in 1 vol. 6s.

"A biography of the beautiful and unhappy Queen, more satisfactory than any we have yet met with."—*Daily News.*

RECOLLECTIONS OF SOCIETY IN FRANCE AND ENGLAND. By Lady Clementina Davies. 2nd Edition. 2 v.

"Two charming volumes, full of the most interesting matter."—*Post.*

THE EXILES AT ST. GERMAINS. By the Author of "The Ladye Shakerley." 1 vol. 7s. 6d. bound.

THE NEW AND POPULAR NOVELS.
PUBLISHED BY HURST & BLACKETT.

A SYLVAN QUEEN. By the Author of "Rachel's Secret," &c. 3 vols.

LILY OF THE VALLEY. By Mrs. RANDOLPH, Author of "Gentianella," &c. 3 vols.

YOUNG LORD PENRITH. By JOHN BERWICK HARWOOD, Author of "Lady Flavia," &c. 3 vols.

"Throughout this novel there is an abundance of well-written passages, in which force and brightness prevail, whilst the descriptions of scenery are as vividly interesting as every other detail is exciting."—*Messenger.*

IN THE SWEET SPRING-TIME. By Mrs. MAC-QUOID, Author of "Patty," &c. 3 vols.

"A most interesting story of domestic life, written in Mrs. Macquoid's best style. It abounds with dramatic situations, and is not wanting in pathos and humour. It is a delightful and refreshing book, in every way deserving of popularity, and worthy of its author's reputation."—*Morning Post.*

"A bright and pleasant tale. There are few living novelists who know better how to tell a love-story than Mrs. Macquoid. The quiet grace and tenderness of her style seem to lend themselves most readily to such a theme, and she has exceptional skill in depicting and analysing the finer and subtler shades of character and emotion."—*Scotsman.*

THE GREATEST HEIRESS IN ENGLAND. By MRS. OLIPHANT, Author of "Chronicles of Carlingford," &c. *Second Edition.* 3 vols.

"'The Greatest Heiress in England' should add to Mrs. Oliphant's reputation. It is noticeably good among the great number of her good novels. The story runs along pleasantly, and maintains the reader's interest throughout."—*Athenæum.*

"This book is a delightful one—fresh, interesting, wholesome, and well written. It deserves to take rank among the best works of the author."—*Examiner.*

"There is a great deal of Mrs. Oliphant's best humour and cleverness in this novel. Her great store of observation and power of amusing description are largely displayed."—*Daily News.*

FRIEND AND LOVER. By IZA DUFFUS HARDY, Author of "Glencairn," &c. 3 vols.

"A powerful story, well worth reading. The plot is ingenious, original, and yet perfectly natural. Miss Hardy's sketches of character are truthful, vivid and graphic. It is decidedly one of the best written books of the season."—*Post.*

"The best novel Miss Hardy has written."—*John Bull.*

"A remarkable, powerful, and fascinating book."—*Sunday Times.*

LITTLE MISS PRIMROSE. By the Author of "St. Olave's," "The Last of her Line," &c. 3 vols.

"The graceful tone and quality of the work of the author of 'St. Olave's' are well known to novel readers. 'Little Miss Primrose' is a very good example of her manner."—*Academy.*

"The author has succeeded in this charming tale in maintaining her popularity. She has drawn, in the heroine, a delightful character, of exceptional grace and elegance."—*Morning Post.*

THROUGH THE STORM. By CHARLES QUENTIN, Author of "So Young, my Lord, and True." 3 vols.

"There is more than the average of exciting incident in this decidedly interesting tale."—*Athenæum.*

"There certainly is in this story not a little that both interests and pleases the reader."—*Saturday Review.*

THE NEW AND POPULAR NOVELS.
PUBLISHED BY HURST & BLACKETT.

YOUNG MRS. JARDINE. By the Author of "John Halifax, Gentleman." *Second Edition.* 3 vols.

"'Young Mrs. Jardine' is a pretty story, written in pure English."—*The Times.*

"There is much tenderness and good feeling in this book. It is pleasant and wholesome."—*Athenæum.*

"'Young Mrs. Jardine' is a book that all should read. Whilst it is quite the equal of any of its predecessors in elevation of thought and style, it is, perhaps, their superior in interest of plot and dramatic intensity."—*Morning Post.*

SIR JOHN. By the Author of "Anne Dysart." 3 v.

"'Sir John' has abundant interest without any straining after the sensational."—*Athenæum.*

"'Sir John' is pleasantly written. The author shows a grasp of character and power of expression of no mean order."—*Examiner.*

RECORDS OF A STORMY LIFE. By the Author of "Recommended to Mercy," &c. 3 vols.

"This book shows decided skill in the delineation of character, and it contains scenes of no little force and pathos."—*The Times.*

"This story has merit, and is decidedly interesting."—*Morning Post.*

GODWYN'S ORDEAL. By Mrs. J. K. SPENDER, Author of "Parted Lives," &c. 3 vols.

"Novel readers owe Mrs. Spender a debt of gratitude for her book. The interest undoubtedly centres in the heroine herself, who is a charming creation."—*Athenæum.*

"This story is pleasantly written, intelligent and earnest."—*Pall Mall Gazette.*

FALSE HEARTS AND TRUE. By Mrs. ALEXANDER FRASER, Author of "A Fatal Passion," &c. 3 vols.

"This work is well calculated to enhance the reputation of Mrs. Fraser as one of our most accomplished novelists. Few readers will fail to be charmed with the easy, pleasant style of the author."—*Post.*

THE HONOURABLE ELLA. By the EARL of DESART, Author of "Kelverdale." *Second Edition.* 3 vols.

"Lord Desart's humour, vivacity, and witty comparisons make his pages sparkle, and give the reader many a pleasant laugh."—*Athenæum.*

ROSE MERVYN. By ANNE BEALE, Author of "Fay Arlington," &c. 3 vols.

"A good novel. The story steadily develops in interest to the close, and Rose, the heroine, is charming."—*Spectator.*

MADELON LEMOINE. By Mrs. LEITH ADAMS, Author of "Winstowe," &c. 3 vols.

"'Madelon Lemoine' is a carefully written book—thoughtful, pleasant, and high toned. The plot of the story is well worked out."—*Athenæum.*

ORANGE LILY. By the Author of "Queenie." 2 v.

"This story is told with both pathos and humour."—*Athenæum.*

"This is a really charming story, one which, by simple power of description and vivid presentment of character, arrests and holds fast the attention."—*Spectator.*

DORCAS. By GEORGIANA M. CRAIK. 3 vols.

"Miss Craik's new novel is clever. Her women are all pleasantly fresh and real."—*Athenæum.*

Under the Especial Patronage of Her Majesty.

Published annually, in One Vol., royal 8vo, with the Arms beautifully engraved, handsomely bound, with gilt edges, price 31s. 6d.

LODGE'S PEERAGE
AND BARONETAGE,
CORRECTED BY THE NOBILITY.

THE FORTY-NINTH EDITION FOR 1880 IS NOW READY.

LODGE'S PEERAGE AND BARONETAGE is acknowledged to be the most complete, as well as the most elegant, work of the kind. As an established and authentic authority on all questions respecting the family histories, honours, and connections of the titled aristocracy, no work has ever stood so high. It is published under the especial patronage of Her Majesty, and is annually corrected throughout, from the personal communications of the Nobility. It is the only work of its class in which, *the type being kept constantly standing*, every correction is made in its proper place to the date of publication, an advantage which gives it supremacy over all its competitors. Independently of its full and authentic information respecting the existing Peers and Baronets of the realm, the most sedulous attention is given in its pages to the collateral branches of the various noble families, and the names of many thousand individuals are introduced, which do not appear in other records of the titled classes. For its authority, correctness, and facility of arrangement, and the beauty of its typography and binding, the work is justly entitled to the place it occupies on the tables of Her Majesty and the Nobility.

LIST OF THE PRINCIPAL CONTENTS.

Historical View of the Peerage.
Parliamentary Roll of the House of Lords.
English, Scotch, and Irish Peers, in their orders of Precedence.
Alphabetical List of Peers of Great Britain and the United Kingdom, holding superior rank in the Scotch or Irish Peerage.
Alphabetical list of Scotch and Irish Peers, holding superior titles in the Peerage of Great Britain and the United Kingdom.
A Collective list of Peers, in their order of Precedence.
Table of Precedency among Men.
Table of Precedency among Women.
The Queen and the Royal Family.
Peers of the Blood Royal.
The Peerage, alphabetically arranged.
Families of such Extinct Peers as have left Widows or Issue.
Alphabetical List of the Surnames of all the Peers.

The Archbishops and Bishops of England and Ireland.
The Baronetage alphabetically arranged.
Alphabetical List of Surnames assumed by members of Noble Families.
Alphabetical List of the Second Titles of Peers, usually borne by their Eldest Sons.
Alphabetical Index to the Daughters of Dukes, Marquises, and Earls, who, having married Commoners, retain the title of Lady before their own Christian and their Husband's Surnames.
Alphabetical Index to the Daughters of Viscounts and Barons, who, having married Commoners, are styled Honourable Mrs.; and, in case of the husband being a Baronet or Knight, Hon. Lady.
A List of the Orders of Knighthood.
Mottoes alphabetically arranged and translated.

"This work is the most perfect and elaborate record of the living and recently deceased members of the Peerage of the Three Kingdoms as it stands at this day. It is a most useful publication. We are happy to bear testimony to the fact that scrupulous accuracy is a distinguishing feature of this book."—*Times.*

"Lodge's Peerage must supersede all other works of the kind, for two reasons: first, it is on a better plan; and secondly, it is better executed. We can safely pronounce it to be the readiest, the most useful, and exactest of modern works on the subject."—*Spectator.*

"A work of great value. It is the most faithful record we possess of the aristocracy of the day."—*Post.*

"The best existing, and, we believe, the best possible Peerage. It is the standard authority on the subject."—*Standard.*

10. THE OLD COURT SUBURB. By LEIGH HUNT.

"A delightful book, that will be welcome to all readers, and most welcome to those who have a love for the best kinds of reading."—*Examiner.*

11. MARGARET AND HER BRIDESMAIDS.

"We recommend all who are in search of a fascinating novel to read this work for themselves. They will find it well worth their while. There are a freshness and originality about it quite charming."—*Athenæum.*

12. THE OLD JUDGE. By SAM SLICK.

"The publications included in this Library have all been of good quality; many give information while they entertain, and of that class the book before us is a specimen. The manner in which the Cheap Editions forming the series is produced, deserves especial mention. The paper and print are unexceptionable; there is a steel engraving in each volume, and the outsides of them will satisfy the purchaser who likes to see books in handsome uniform."—*Examiner.*

13. DARIEN. By ELIOT WARBURTON.

"This last production of the author of 'The Crescent and the Cross' has the same elements of a very wide popularity. It will please its thousands."—*Globe.*

14. FAMILY ROMANCE.

BY SIR BERNARD BURKE, ULSTER KING OF ARMS.

"It were impossible to praise too highly this most interesting book."—*Standard.*

15. THE LAIRD OF NORLAW. By MRS. OLIPHANT.

"The 'Laird of Norlaw' fully sustains the author's high reputation."—*Sunday Times.*

16. THE ENGLISHWOMAN IN ITALY.

"Mrs. Gretton's book is interesting, and full of opportune instruction."—*Times.*

17. NOTHING NEW.

BY THE AUTHOR OF "JOHN HALIFAX, GENTLEMAN."

"'Nothing New' displays all those superior merits which have made 'John Halifax' one of the most popular works of the day."—*Post.*

18. FREER'S LIFE OF JEANNE D'ALBRET.

"Nothing can be more interesting than Miss Freer's story of the life of Jeanne D'Albret, and the narrative is as trustworthy as it is attractive."—*Post.*

19. THE VALLEY OF A HUNDRED FIRES.

BY THE AUTHOR OF "MARGARET AND HER BRIDESMAIDS."

"If asked to classify this work, we should give it a place between 'John Halifax' and 'The Caxtons.'"—*Standard.*

20. THE ROMANCE OF THE FORUM.

BY PETER BURKE, SERGEANT AT LAW.

"A work of singular interest, which can never fail to charm."—*Illustrated News.*

21. ADELE. By JULIA KAVANAGH.

"'Adele' is the best work we have read by Miss Kavanagh; it is a charming story, full of delicate character-painting."—*Athenæum.*

22. STUDIES FROM LIFE.

BY THE AUTHOR OF "JOHN HALIFAX, GENTLEMAN."

"These 'Studies from Life' are remarkable for graphic power and observation. The book will not diminish the reputation of the accomplished author."—*Saturday Review.*

23. GRANDMOTHER'S MONEY.

"We commend 'Grandmother's Money' to readers in search of a good novel. The characters are true to human nature, and the story is interesting."—*Athenæum.*

24. A BOOK ABOUT DOCTORS.
BY J. C. JEAFFRESON.
" A delightful book."—*Athenæum.* " A book to be read and re-read; fit for the study as well as the drawing-room table and the circulating library."—*Lancet.*

25. NO CHURCH.
" We advise all who have the opportunity to read this book."—*Athenæum.*

26. MISTRESS AND MAID.
BY THE AUTHOR OF " JOHN HALIFAX, GENTLEMAN."
" A good wholesome book, gracefully written, and as pleasant to read as it is instructive."—*Athenæum.* " A charming tale charmingly told."—*Standard.*

27. LOST AND SAVED. By HON. MRS. NORTON.
" 'Lost and Saved' will be read with eager interest. It is a vigorous novel."—*Times.* " A novel of rare excellence. It is Mrs. Norton's best prose work."—*Examiner.*

28. LES MISERABLES. By VICTOR HUGO.
AUTHORISED COPYRIGHT ENGLISH TRANSLATION.
" The merits of 'Les Miserables' do not merely consist in the conception of it as a whole; it abounds with details of unequalled beauty. M. Victor Hugo has stamped upon every page the hall-mark of genius."—*Quarterly Review.*

29. BARBARA'S HISTORY. By AMELIA B. EDWARDS.
" It is not often that we light upon a novel of so much merit and interest as 'Barbara's History.' It is a work conspicuous for taste and literary culture. It is a very graceful and charming book, with a well-managed story, clearly-cut characters, and sentiments expressed with an exquisite elocution. It is a book which the world will like."—*Times.*

30. LIFE OF THE REV. EDWARD IRVING.
BY MRS. OLIPHANT.
" A good book on a most interesting theme."—*Times.*
" A truly interesting and most affecting memoir. Irving's Life ought to have a niche in every gallery of religious biography. There are few lives that will be fuller of instruction, interest, and consolation."—*Saturday Review.*

31. ST. OLAVE'S.
" This charming novel is the work of one who possesses a great talent for writing, as well as experience and knowledge of the world. '—*Athenæum.*

32. SAM SLICK'S AMERICAN HUMOUR.
" Dip where you will into this lottery of fun, you are sure to draw out a prize."—*Post.*

33. CHRISTIAN'S MISTAKE.
BY THE AUTHOR OF " JOHN HALIFAX, GENTLEMAN."
" A more charming story has rarely been written. Even if tried by the standard of the Archbishop of York, we should expect that even he would pronounce 'Christian's Mistake' a novel without a fault."—*Times.*

34. ALEC FORBES OF HOWGLEN.
BY GEORGE MAC DONALD, LL.D.
" No account of this story would give any idea of the profound interest that pervades the work from the first page to the last."—*Athenæum.*

35. AGNES. By MRS. OLIPHANT.
" 'Agnes' is a novel superior to any of Mrs. Oliphant's former works."—*Athenæum.* " A story whose pathetic beauty will appeal irresistibly to all readers."—*Post.*

36. A NOBLE LIFE.
BY THE AUTHOR OF " JOHN HALIFAX, GENTLEMAN."
" This is one of those pleasant tales in which the author of 'John Halifax' speaks out of a generous heart the purest truths of life."—*Examiner.*

HURST & BLACKETT'S STANDARD LIBRARY

37. NEW AMERICA. By HEPWORTH DIXON.

" A very interesting book. Mr. Dixon has written thoughtfully and well."—*Times*.
"We recommend every one who feels any interest in human nature to read Mr. Dixon's very interesting book."—*Saturday Review*.

38. ROBERT FALCONER.

BY GEORGE MAC DONALD, LL.D.

"'Robert Falconer' is a work brimful of life and humour and of the deepest human interest. It is a book to be returned to again and again for the deep and searching knowledge it evinces of human thoughts and feelings."—*Athenæum*.

39. THE WOMAN'S KINGDOM.

BY THE AUTHOR OF "JOHN HALIFAX, GENTLEMAN."

"'The Woman's Kingdom' sustains the author's reputation as a writer of the purest and noblest kind of domestic stories.—*Athenæum*.

40. ANNALS OF AN EVENTFUL LIFE.

BY GEORGE WEBBE DASENT, D.C.L.

"A racy, well-written, and original novel. The interest never flags. The whole work sparkles with wit and humour."—*Quarterly Review*.

41. DAVID ELGINBROD. By GEORGE MAC DONALD.

"The work of a man of genius. It will attract the highest class of readers."—*Times*.

42. A BRAVE LADY.

BY THE AUTHOR OF "JOHN HALIFAX, GENTLEMAN."

"A very good novel; a thoughtful, well-written book, showing a tender sympathy with human nature, and permeated by a pure and noble spirit."—*Examiner*.

43. HANNAH.

BY THE AUTHOR OF "JOHN HALIFAX, GENTLEMAN."

" A very pleasant, healthy story, well and artistically told. The book is sure of a wide circle of readers. The character of Hannah is one of rare beauty."—*Standard*.

44. SAM SLICK'S AMERICANS AT HOME.

"This is one of the most amusing books that we ever read."—*Standard*.

45. THE UNKIND WORD.

BY THE AUTHOR OF "JOHN HALIFAX, GENTLEMAN."

"The author of 'John Halifax' has written many fascinating stories, but we can call to mind nothing from her pen that has a more enduring charm than the graceful sketches in this work."—*United Service Magazine*.

46. A ROSE IN JUNE. By MRS. OLIPHANT.

"'A Rose in June' is as pretty as its title. The story is one of the best and most touching which we owe to the industry and talent of Mrs. Oliphant, and may hold its own with even 'The Chronicles of Carlingford.'"—*Times*.

47. MY LITTLE LADY. By E. F. POYNTER.

"There is a great deal of fascination about this book. The author writes in a clear, unaffected style; she has a decided gift for depicting character, while the descriptions of scenery convey a distinct pictorial impression to the reader."—*Times*.

48. PHŒBE, JUNIOR. By MRS. OLIPHANT.

"This novel shows great knowledge of human nature. The interest goes on growing to the end. Phœbe is excellently drawn."—*Times*.

49. LIFE OF MARIE ANTOINETTE.

BY PROFESSOR CHARLES DUKE YONGE.

" A work of remarkable merit and interest, which will, we doubt not, become the most popular English history of Marie Antoinette."—*Spectator*.
"This book is well written, and of thrilling interest."—*Academy*,